DESTINY
—OR—
FATE

A TALE FROM THE "OUTER WORLD COLLECTION"

Artica Burr

OTHER BOOKS BY ARTICA BURR

Hockey Legend Myth and Verse

(Trafford Publishing, Canada)

Billy Bender and the Red Hot Ants

(Artica Burr Publications, USA)

Precious Bloodline

(Artica Burr Publications, USA)

Monty's Magnificent Hairball

(Artica Burr Publications, USA)

PROLOGUE

The timeline unfolds near Buffalo, New York, during year three in "New Amerika," after the last shreds of prior United States of America Inc. had taken a final fall from operational and financial grace. Immediately afterward, due to the chaos, a Revolutionary War for Freedom ripped America further asunder. That unrest had created the perfect timing for the United World Nation, the UWN, to step in and enter the fray. The news commentators were advised to refer to the war as a Civil War, not the Revolutionary War against the government that it truly was.

Being isolated into sections within town limits reinforced the stranglehold of the flow of fresh information. According to the single remaining news outlet, a Civil War still raged on, but locations where such combat was occurring were never disclosed. The clever ploy of only partial war news coverage kept the slow-burning candle of hope flickering and the masses quietly waiting.

The boldest in the neighborhoods clung to the expectation that freedom was only a future confrontation away, waiting to join the confrontation if and when the war approached their town. Communication methods, other rights, and assets were being siphoned away one after another. Some of the docile workers, who still fostered an underlying unwavering determination, shared their thoughts written on napkins in their workplace cafeteria, passed them on, and at the end of their meal break, all the notes were quickly dissolved or flushed away.

For the welfare of all concerned, or so they professed, the United World Nation had inflicted their social rule and dictates known as the 'Semblance of Order' upon the general public. Every added regulation was sugar-coated as being for the common good. During the final years of America, the powers in control discovered that creating heavy-handed fear, treating the masses to lockdowns, demanding a ban on firearms, and suggesting that Jesus endorsed every mandated pharmaceutical was ineffectual in the long run. Voluntary containment for the greater good, diet control, the looming threat of the loss of their homes, unavailability of ammunition, and lack of independent transportation yielded far better behavior results.

Gone were science, history, and all but basic eighth-grade education. There was no longer one national language, which undoubtedly contributed to some violent misunderstandings. Formal pillars of education now consisted of learning to follow instructions, check off a form, and print a personal name and identification number. Elementary students voraciously studied the 'Semblance of Order' regulations which enabled them to effectively join the daily Youth Cadet Patrol and issue tickets for violations to those in their neighborhood. The points the students earned for each ticket were credited towards prepaid vacation days from which the youths did or did not return. Some youth cadets had come to perfect the silent, fine art of bribery for black market items or extra food.

Secondary School had simply become the final rung of a sorting ground for future workers, soldiers, or disposables. The student's level of voluntary compliance was the graduation or failure scoring factor. After that milestone or failure, the graduates were no longer allowed to live with their families. They disappeared into dormitories located near their assigned workplace, the military, or a place loosely termed "somewhere."

In the penetrating darkness of night, up and down the streets, one by one, the homes were being emptied of the established residents. By language and conduct definitions, multiple new residents who moved into the vacated homes were clearly selected gang members and thugs who had rushed to the border some time ago and entered America bare of vetting. Those who still remained living in government encampments teetered between their secretive past and an unforeseen future. At first, America had proposed that its citizens open their hearts and minds and share their homes with unregistered newcomers; however, the public expressed a heavily diminished sense of trust, and the candy-laced suggestion quickly fell flat.

Other new residents created a bubbling brew of suspicions. These peculiar new move-ins lurked outside in the darkness after curfew, with odd, unsettling, and, as some awkwardly worded it, these Newcomers presented with strange, alien-type physical behaviors.

Questions loomed in the heads of the initially established residents. Was a total population replacement plan in play? Had they waited too long and lost any window of opportunity for freedom? Was there still somewhere to escape to in the next town, city, or state? What would be their fate? When and where would they themselves be taken to the ever-undefined "somewhere"?

How can you detect the absolute truth? Simple. It's more than you bargained for.

CONTENTS

Prologue	iv
Contents	ix
Chapter 1	11
Chapter 2	25
Chapter 3	40
Chapter 4	49
Chapter 5	53
Chapter 6	63
Chapter 7	70
Chapter 8	84
Chapter 9	93
Chapter 10	100
Chapter 11	109
Chapter 12	117
Chapter 13	129
Chapter 14	135
Chapter 15	140

Chapter 16		146
Chapter 17		156
Chapter 18		166
Chapter 19		187
Chapter 20		196
Chapter 21		204
Chapter 22		218
Chapter 23		223
Chapter 24		230
Chapter 25		236
Chapter 26		246
About the Author		255

CHAPTER ONE

On Friday at high noon, the harsh rasp of the end-of-workday buzzer pierced the air and echoed down the halls. The workers dutifully exited the study hall, which replaced what had been a gymnasium in prior years. They silently filed into the cafeteria for their meager yet welcome customary end-of-the-week warm bowl of vegetable soup and crackers, after which they would all trudge home in the fog, cleansed of the work week by today's expected light spring rain. A bowl of soup that was scarce of vegetables was the worker's study day's pay. For the sake of the common good, a four-hour review of the government's 'Semblance of Order Regulations' had replaced the paid Friday workday in order to ensure the workers were up to date on all the ever-changing regulations applicable to citizens.

In a makeshift fashion, Five Star Energy had converted an idle high school into their robotic parts factory and repair facility. A week now consisted of four days of paid labor, one half-day of study concerning regulations, and one day of rest. The United World Nation's abrupt new regulation of a six-day calendar week was a difficult adjustment for the masses, especially for the children. Sunday had been swept into the dustbin of history. It had held too many religious connotations to suit the dastardly vision of the UWN.

Jules took a place in the cafeteria line, awaiting her tray. The pit of her stomach was churning like the rhythm of her clothes washer as she awaited the end-of-month termination results. The work team had found three completely useless joints that the robots had designed. The robotic manufacturing arm parts that her team evaluated were highly valued and assembled by robots. The United World Nation boasted of the need to replace human workers because their new robots were touted as infallible. The team had found errors they were unable to correct, and with due regret, they had to scrap the three massively faulty pieces the robots had created. Jules had never heard of such a robotic significant work error being made. Her team's termination could hang in the balance necessary to politically cover for a lofty robotic mistake. The work team had taken the time to print an explanation concerning the proposed decision to scrap the parts in question. Steeling herself to accept her fate, Jules slid her tray along the serving bars adjacent to the counter and moved forward as the lunch line progressed.

"You're it today, Jules Martain," the busy cafeteria worker whispered as her nimble fingers slipped a few extra crackers on Jules' tray and ladled soup into her bowl. Stirring to the bottom of the pot, the server located a few extra carrots to add to Jules' bowl. Here's the team's Labor Reduction Notice," she said as she laid a crisply folded sheet of paper onto Jules' tray. The server's hand remained on top of the report.

Jules struggled against it, but her hands began to tremble as she balanced the tray on the rungs along the counter area. Last month, she had seen this same server sympathetically pat the hand of a worker who was on her way to being terminated. Jules shakingly reached to pick up the report. The server rested her hand on Jules while forming an OK sign with her fingers. A spark of life seeped into Jules' eyes as her look of relief met that of the cafeteria worker. The exchanged visual contact measured the depth of kindling hope they shared within.

"Thanks for the carrot increase, but the monthly reports always make me so nervous," Jules responded, wincing as she glanced at the folded Labor Reduction Notice with her name on it. Relief touched the inside of her stomach when the cafeteria worker gave her a confident nod. Jules suspected that once the soup was simmering, out of curiosity, the kitchen workers all read the contents of the Labor Reduction Notices. The reports were never concealed in envelopes.

Each team of workers had a strictly assigned cafeteria seating. On Fridays, six gel ink pens graced the center of each table. Jules' chair scraped the bare floor with a grating noise as she moved it and proceeded to take her seat. The sound was reminiscent of Jules' high school past, but the cafeteria lacked the normal chatter of youthful years. The conversation was restricted to each table as seated.

After Jules breathed a sigh of semi-relief, she freed up her tight work headband, shook her head, and fluffed her dark blond hair until it fell upon her shoulders. As rules required, she slipped her logoed Five Star headband back in place. Being "it" meant that Jules was to lead her team's discussion about the indoctrination class they had just attended or announce to her team that their work effort was no longer required.

Once seated around the table, the team's tension concerning the Labor Reduction Report was obvious. It was a repetitive reaction on each last Friday of the month, but in this case, even though they had all agreed that those particular parts had to be rejected rather than fixed, the team's stress level was on an upward curve due to their rejection of the almighty robotic errors they had found. All eyes were focused on Jules when she inhaled, sighed, and unfolded the team's Labor Reduction Notice.

The air in the room always felt thick with anticipation until every table opened its report in turn. To date, the team Jules was on had not received a one-time warning that usually indicated a team's future dismissal. No production report quantities were ever shared by the management. Jules read the report aloud, "Your team's production was up to standard for the last month, and therefore, no termination was necessary." The team sighed in unison with relief, and as the report circulated around the table, Jules watched each of them yield a muted smile in turn.

"Maybe our written explanation has saved us," Jules quietly remarked.

A burst of distressed moans of anguish echoed from across the room. Everyone at that table appeared shaken and fraught with anxiety. All of them abruptly left their soup behind and rapidly exited the cafeteria, likely into the not-so-welcoming arms of plant security. That particular work team had been positioned adjacent to their team on the plant work floor. For several weeks, Jules had noticed that their workstation had progressively buzzed with confusion over the decision-making process. Their loss of the ability to locate parts problems and determine the repairs needed had multiplied like bees congregating near a hive. Management always terminated whole teams at once to include the slackers as well as the innocent rather than focus on selecting problem individuals. Dismissal was always one grand swat with a sting for all provided. The workers all depended on their jobs not only to prove their worth to society but also to put food on their own tables. AI corporate management had always remained faceless. It depended on surveillance and its production tallies. In a bitter twist, it allowed the workers the privilege of dismissing other employees via the monthly issued Labor Reduction Report.

Jules spoke quietly, "Hopefully, this means that management has accepted our judgment that the parts we rejected were unfixable. The failure of the robot's performance concerning the manufacture of those parts is best not repeated by any of us. Not rejecting those parts could have been a costly error for Five Star as a company. AI management never says it because praise is foreign to their thinking, but we know our art of human cooperation makes us the best work team Five Star Energy has on the floor. On that note, congrats to each of us."

Any glance her team made across the workplace floor, and they were well aware of how well they coordinated their team's workflow, but Jules always latched onto any occasion to use positive encouragement. Her few years of teaching in a classroom had perfected a technique that always reinforced unity. The team could rest easy for their one day off and then return to hopefully fulfilling satisfactory quotas to be accumulated for next month's looming report. The unspoken question concerned the abyss of what happened to those who lost their job.

"Whose turn is it to tack this up on their fridge door?" Jules asked while placing the report in the center of the table.

After a moment of silence, Jim drawled his response, "If it's OK with you all, posting this might earn my wife's forgiveness for not fixing the faucet until tonight." With quick smiles, all of the team members nodded yes.

Jules was the only woman on her work team of six. All the guys were great team players. It was nothing short of a fortunate flip of fate that they all were accidentally jettisoned onto the same work team. Jules knew the team members fairly well since she had taught some of their children back when New Amerika was America. She had been an elementary teacher at the local school. When they saw each other at the hiring assembly, they had naturally grouped together to greet one another. When the intercom had directed all workers to move to workstations, they had moved in unison to the same workstation. All of the teams, in effect, self-selected their composition, damning themselves, to success or failure, perhaps on some age-old birds of a feather theory. If termination reared its ugly head, they could only blame their initial choice of feathering their work nest poorly.

Jules still had dreams where she was back in the classroom with little upturned, trusting, second-grade faces gazing back at her, enjoying their school day. Her very best memory was the Mother's Day floral cards she and her students had made. The children were so elated to report how much their mothers or grandmothers liked the gift.

Jules had failed to be as politically correct as the confining UWN curriculum required. It was a comedown losing her teaching job and becoming a low-rung factory worker, but at least she trusted those she now worked with. Four were married, and she even knew their wives from progress meetings at school functions. Peter was the only single guy on the team. Jules had known him since High School, and he was always quick to cover extra load if anyone seemed a bit tired. He was fast friends with Micheal Bennett, a sailor whom Jules had dated during a leave from his military unit right before the political tightrope snapped and New Amerika was born.

Every Tuesday, Jules gave the guys a heads-up if she wanted to shower after work. They all respectfully waited patiently for any women to finish before they entered the one shower for all facilities that the plant provided, which was part of the prior boy's locker room. Jules only showered at work once a week just to keep her home water allowance low enough to allow for the water needed by her precious onions, lettuce, bush cucumbers, and cherry tomatoes, which she stealthily nurtured. She had stocked up on growing supplies before the town isolation lockdowns occurred. Although even as a child, she liked to keep things on schedule and in balance, the lockdown regulations had increasingly created an overbearing strain on Jules' everyday life.

Jules perceived that, as usual, some notes the team would pass would address the forbidden subject of the Civil War, as the government called it, rather than the Revolutionary War it truly was. Relative team discussion was mandatory each week after the day's class. Today, it would be her responsibility to discreetly dispose of any off-work topic napkin notes. Class questions or comments could be faithfully deposited in the ordinary trash can, but off-subject comments had to be discreetly disposed of. It was fortunate that the napkins provided dissolved the minute they hit any kind of liquid. There surely were no lingering moments in the lavatory using the quick liquefying toilet paper either. It was clear that AI failed to understand the basic sanitary requirements that lavatory use required.

As things momentarily stood, at least money was still printed on durable paper, although with prices soaring, money had its own method of vanishing rapidly. The idea of digital currency had tumbled by the wayside when the decision was introduced to strip the public of cell phones and data devices. The powers that be had hit the brick wall of achieving it all. Digital currency would enable contact with the outside world and tracing of all cash flow, even theirs. Cash was still king. The public could feast on an illusion of some freedom, but only legally used items could be purchased from the town store. As an afterthought, buying from or exchanging items with a neighbor had suddenly become illegal and was considered dealing in black market items. It was still legal to exchange used gifts. On the Saturday before a neighbor's birthday, one was besieged by close living residents touting pillowcases fully stuffed with items to barter with.

Jules softly cleared her throat. To catch the team's attention, she rhythmically tapped her spoon on her soup bowl. "Ok. May I have the team's attention? Let's get done so we can head home. So, what is your least favorite regulation discussed today? Write a comment on the napkin and then pass it to your left around the table. If you agree with a comment, then just put +1 next to the comment. We will do a two-time pass-around for comments and one final, so all the comments are fully shared. Let's go, go, go before our soup gets completely cold."

All of the gel ink pens busily hit the napkin as it moved rapidly around the table back to Jules.

"No one likes the fact that they are going to start monitoring our conversations while we work. Our team's conversations are always concerning what we are working on, so it won't matter to our team, but I personally find it annoying too," Jules responded while adding her own +1. "I love the suggestion of forcing them to overhear a daily riddle or a joke. One thing that disrupts an adversary, if I may suggest AI management might be such, is laughter. Some of you seem to wonder if management may decide to raise our quota of items produced without disclosing it to us."

"I would like to address all of our team on those matters." Jim murmured in his slow-paced manner. A security guard quietly entered the room. His attention was focused on Jim. It was risky and unusual for anyone to express the need to speak their thoughts. Jim was aware of the guard's interest, but he still persisted. "I think what I have to say is too long to waste everyone's time while I write it down. I used to be a Production Manager elsewhere. It stands to reason that since AI is in a learning mode, it does not know what quota to set without, by their rules, risking losing all the production teams at the same time. They never give us a specific quota. By that token, our team may even be setting the quota.

"AI does not understand what human coordination is and how it affects production. Theoretically, it wants to erase the need for human contribution, but human harmony is exactly what drives success as far as team productivity. If I am right in my thinking, management is still unsure what tally to require of each of the teams or why there is a variance from one team to another. It needs to look at an all over summary goal of productivity combining all the teams. It only takes one individual to foul up a team's production, and for any number of reasons, that might be an off day or week for a team member.

"But my real concern is I am noticing workers on some of the other teams are losing their ability to think things through on the job; thus, they drag their whole team down with them. While humans think as individuals, AI thinks of situations as a composite. A production manager's job was to see a problem with workflow and resolve it. We had a daily report to file for management. I think that each team needs a lead person. Once good lead people are active on each team, if needed selective worker replacement could occur. That's my overall view of things and the comment I offer." By the time Jim finished speaking to the table, he noticed that the security guard had quietly backed out of the room.

"Interesting," Jules said. That would save time on retraining whole teams. Can we all vote on that?" Jules passed the napkin again. "Add any further comments."

This time, when the napkin returned to Jules, it reflected that they all agreed with Jim. It also was noted that someone was concerned that additional diet restrictions were going to start very soon, with three of the +1's being added. All had voted for riddles or jokes being told. The word "over" was lettered on the bottom of the napkin. Jules flipped the napkin face down.

Last night, I heard gunshots, maybe 20 miles or so to the south. Civil War? was written with two +1's. Another penned comment was that it could be just gang members, with a single +1. Jules jumped slightly in her seat when she saw the final comment. What Jules viewed on the napkin was, "Can I walk you home since I can't meet you in the shower?"

Jules' sapphire blue eyes snapped. Her rapid glance around the table surveyed the team members. Everyone was questioning her look except Peter, who was sitting next to her to her right, stirring his soup. Jim sitting to her left, took the napkin out of her hand and began the final pass around. He let out a low laugh, and the napkin rapidly sped around the table, with each recipient stifling a snicker along the way.

When the napkin returned to Peter, he addressed his comment. "I was just kidding you, Jules. Let's eat our soup. Think of it as an offhand compliment. I realize the shower remark was out of line, but seeing the look on your face was priceless. I assume you're still waiting for word about my buddy Michael, who was due to return from his military duty over a year ago. I respect that," Peter said with his winning smile. He looked into Jules' wide blue eyes, winced, quickly broke his crackers into his soup, and turned his close attention to his bowl and spoon.

Jules laughed lightly. "OK. You got me good, and I get it, Peter," she responded. "This new government works hard at sweeping away our humor and casual conversation. I haven't heard a word from Michael. If you hear anything good, bad, or indifferent, please do let me know so I can artfully stop the infernal internal wondering. I hate loose ends.

"I'm glad we all had a chance to share a bit of humor, even if it was at my expense. I honestly have forgotten every joke or riddle I ever knew and, at moments, how to just plain laugh at myself. Maybe AI management can come to understand the value of humor. Maybe not, but let's give it a try. We can start at a low classroom second-grade level and build from there. I'll have one of those ready for Monday."

While the rest were finishing their soup, Peter spoke to Jules under his breath. "I did just find out some information on Michael. After over two years of barely hearing from him, I'm going to guess we are no longer best buddies. It never was that way before. I heard from him once a month before this. The military can change a man. I can catch up to you by the Town Park if you want and share the info." He waited for her answer. She nodded a yes.

Jules left some liquid in the bottom of her soup bowl. When the napkin returned to her, she watched it dissolve into nothingness after the napkin was nestled into her bowl. She had an uncomfortable premonition that her friendship and potential relationship with Michael had met a similar fate.

CHAPTER TWO

Jules began her walk home in a thick visual fog with a gentle mist of rain. Images of dark tree trunks with bare, twisted branches emerged along the sidewalk as she progressed onward. The dead or dying trunks stood like haunting soldiers, still testifying to America's past, when they were free to sink their roots, grow, and prosper. It was the mid-month of March when Spring used to systematically begin before the United World Nation, in their interest to own everything, seized possession of the four seasons. The powers that be, with their invisible hand, merged the seasons into one endless, eternal weather cycle.

Jules immediately vacated her bitter-tinged mindset when she concentrated on recalling the sweet moments from the past and then managing to shunt the reflections of her current reality onto her back burner. She vowed to try to keep her thoughts positive throughout her one weekly day away from the factory, but each week, it had become progressively difficult to achieve that goal. She found her thoughts searching for a way to escape the weight of her reality.

At least at this point in time, they could not steal her memories. The blooming trees in her neighborhood, which had provided such a peaceful, lovely touch and a seasonal picture of America, now looked barren and foreboding. Still, in her mind's eye, she could recall their glory. Flowering crabapples had dotted the whole town. Outside the library in the Village, the delicate pink-blooming cherry tree petals would cascade across the open book Jules read while she sat on the bench beneath, turning page after page. Part of the spring season in her neighborhood had always been the permeating sweet, intoxicating scent of the lilacs and the songs of the courting birds as they welcomed another spring season and readied to nest.

Her father had hung a small but tall white birdhouse outside the dining room window for the same little wren every year. Together, they both had repainted it several times. The little wren looked for that nesting place year after year. Once he hung the birdhouse up, she would fly out of nowhere and sit by that birdhouse until a male wren came courting her. He would spread his tail and persistently dance on the branch while singing a tender medley of songs until he won the heart of the little wren, and she agreed he could help her build a nest for their young.

Jules had watched and waited with her mom and dad each morning until they could count the number of young the wrens had faithfully tended to as hatchlings. Once the little ones hopped out of the nest box, it was the male's duty to line up the young on a branch and repeatedly teach them the traditional wren songs until every fledgling got the songs correct. If any of the young missed a single note of the song, he would scold them until they all got it right. It had been delightful viewing their intimate customs, but how they could raise five young wrens in that tiny birdhouse still remained a mystery to Jules.

Robins were the first heralds of the coming spring. They dropped from the sky upon the yard in a flock, chattering as they searched for earthworms, then deciding how many would elect to stay and the number who would vacate into other yards. Some of them chose to build a nest in insane places, hopefully not over a doorway.

One robin made a nest on the ledge under a window right next to her mother's porch swing. Before her mother could remove the nest, the eggs were carefully nestled in the bottom. Things got rather messy once all the young started shooting their droppings over the side of their nest. A piece of cardboard was then faithfully placed on the porch floor to reduce future cleanup. Her mom had tried to remove the nest as soon as it was empty, but the robin quickly reclaimed it by giving quite a talk to her mother's invading hand. Weeks later, the robin laid eggs for yet another set of peepers while sitting on the nest and watching her mother eating breakfast toast while on the porch swing.

Jules recalled how she set up a birdbath with a water-spritzing feature. One of the robins returned every day to soak herself in the birdbath. She remembered calling out to the robin while it sat half-submerged in the water. Jules found herself whispering those exact words out loud, "Enjoy your bath, pretty bird. So sorry your bottom is egg-laying sore." She was eight, and one day at the Farmer's Market, while her mother was buying eggs, she asked a lady how a bird could lay such a hard egg. That night, Jules had announced at the supper table that she knew a special secret about birds. Her parents quickly looked at one another. Then, her mother broke the silence by asking exactly what the special secret was.

Jules backslid into acknowledging what had transpired since. Nature's difficulties began the first year the bio-trees were planted. The balance of nature was rudely interrupted. Climate control quickly waged its war against the area's native trees as well as the planted ornamentals, leaving only the genetically engineered plantings performing as vivid artificial scars upon the landscape.

The public had been advised that birds had found disfavor with the government because they were proven carriers of illness. Jules suspected the birds were dying because of the chemical content of the bio-engineered plantings. Dead and also live bird collection then became the town worker's prominent campaign. A void of eerie silence had fallen upon the yards and parks. The only birds that continued to make their visual presence known were the forbidding vultures that circled and feasted on the dwindling wildlife.

The fog had thinned to a swirling mist, allowing Jules to dream that if it completely cleared, the old America would await her as she awakened from the nightmare of reality. Jules had always shaken her head at how her mother hesitated to throw out her old calendars. Now, Jules hung those calendar pictures on her basement walls to bask in the memory of past historic American seasonal glow.

Jules interrupted her walk home by stopping by the crabapple tree at the entrance to what had been the local bank next to the Town Park. The tree's structure had been an art form, and the shape was still intact. She bent down and pushed the heavy dead weed growth away from the base of the trunk. Defiant small sucker branches were actually pushing outward from the trunk. Upon closer examination, there was a showing of buds forming on several of the lower branches that she could easily reach.

"Wonderful!" Jules said out loud as she reverently touched the persistent growth. "Please keep trying. I'll be checking on your progress after every workday."

The spring bulbs hadn't activated themselves for the past two years. Jules missed the wild, unexpected dots of color they had brought to the neighborhood. This year, during the prior appropriate time period, the temperature fluctuated by over twenty degrees, quite unlike its behavior during the past two years. She hurried over to the stone wall in front of the Town Park. Jules knelt down where she had planted hyacinths five years ago during a Garden Club project. After she tugged some of the overgrowth away, she found that the bulb growth had pushed upward out of the ground and was yielding the formation of buds. Some daffodil greenery had also struggled to the surface. The electricity of excitement surged through Jules. The raw hope that spring would reveal itself once again quickly brought tears to her eyes.

Peter had silently approached the situation and then stood behind Jules. Curiously, he ventured a guess. "What are you looking for? Did you lose something in particular? Perhaps your computer-generated government nose ring fell off into the weeds?"

"I'd be more than pleased if our CGI nose rings were gone for good," Jules answered. "But look, look! I found spring bulbs coming up! Those dips in temperature must have reminded them it's Spring!" Jules' face was lit with excitement when she looked up at Peter.

"Well, be darned, at long last, nature has declared its own Revolutionary War and begun to fight back," Peter answered. "Leave some weeds loosely covering them, and if they bloom, we can pick them all before the town-level party poopers catch on and rip the old garden spot up. Then I bet the Town Board would adorn the spot with bio-engineered crap. They sure don't favor natural living things while they profess to save the planet. Long about now it's a comfort to see anything that used to be. I, for one, sure wish they would reopen the old museum now that I have more time to read, but I guess they are just too busy rewriting the town's history."

"You got that right," Jules answered as she gently brushed the weeds over the bulbs to only partly filter out the sun.

"I hate to remove you from a moment of pleasure, but I came to give you what info I heard about Michael. With no Internet and phones, it's just second-party chatter, but it does make quite a bit of sense.

"Michael and I grew up like brothers, so I've been poking around to find out where he got to because he should be done with his military time. I can't leave this section and get to the location where we used to live, and Michael's mom still lives there. After excessive queries, I found someone who knows Michael's sister. It was the sister who I was looking for, and she doesn't live in our section of town."

Jules stayed quietly seated on the ground, yielding a need-to-know expression.

"We all knew Michael was serving his Navy time at Seneca Lake, where the submarine testing and experimentation goes on. After you both spent his last leave together and his leave was over, I drove him back to Seneca Lake, where he was stationed. He told me how the ships come in from the Atlantic Ocean out East by navigating an underground seaway that continued beyond Seneca Lake. He had heard it connected the Atlantic Ocean to the Pacific Ocean with hubs at many military bases in between. That was news to me. I guess you never know what truly is beneath your feet.

"Since you saw him last, I never heard he got any additional leaves; at least, he never returned for any visits back home. Michael did write to me four months ago. He said that the MQ Reaper Drone the government lost in Lake Ontario in 2013 suddenly was on the military list for recovery. Michael couldn't understand the lapse of time they left the drone down there or why the military would have allowed an inexperienced drone pilot to computer operate a drone worth over a million bucks. The newborn operator claimed that he might have miscalculated, and thus, it crashed in Lake Ontario. He remarked that they have smaller stuff to let a guy learn on. But I put my own four years in the Navy, and wow, did I see more than a few stupid decisions made. So, Michael and I were on the same page with that, but it is what it is.

"A month after that, Michael wrote me and said they were being sent out to take a look at the downed Reaper drone. He was aware that a new drone report showed something else was down there alongside the downed MQ that didn't look to be crash debris from when the MQ went down near the Rocky Scholes. There were to be three divers, Michael being one of them. They were all close to release or re-up time and apprehensive that something might be radioactive where the drone lay. He felt that if they seriously wanted to recover it, 2013 would be a wasteful and long time to wait. I wrote back to him, offering to pick him up since he had said he wasn't going to re-enlist. Michael and I always knew what the other guy was thinking. Neither one of us acknowledged it, but we both knew the downed drone sat in a location called the Mary's Burgh Vortex."

"A vortex like the Bermuda Triangle in Lake Ontario?" Jules queried in disbelief.

"So, they say," Peter said. But it seems to be concentrated just on the right-hand end of the lake.

"Did you find his sister Brenda's friend?" Jules intently asked.

"Yes, finally, and she lived close to our area's limits. Just the day before yesterday, I slipped over to her place after curfew with two loaves of bread in a bag like I was delivering a package." Peter exhaled and then sat down next to Jules.

"I'm afraid we will never get a completely good answer. The Navy told the family that they had sent a small diving boat out on Lake Ontario with a Captain and three divers. The boat was seen on the lake. Early on that night, there was a distress call from the boat, but it was quickly interrupted by static. They did send marine rescue, but they only found an empty boat with the diving gear still all on board. The Navy searched the whole of Lake Ontario with their underwater explorer for two weeks, but they could not find the men. The military is acting like the men went AWOL, but I say it's likely the Mary's Burgh Vortex. Until more transpires, no answer is the right answer, and it's anybody's guess."

Jules' eyes welled with tears of frustration. "No answer is all we have. What are you thinking?"

"Well," Peter answered. "I ruled out the possibility that the military lost the men to radiation while diving because the diving gear was as yet unused, and the Navy guy manning the boat was gone too. They would have to do a thorough search even to consider calling the sailors AWOL, and they did for two weeks. AWOL doesn't make sense in Michael's case or the others.

"I recall that during my time, several guys disappeared just before their duty time was going to be up. Word was they were spun off into the Super Soldier Program. I heard that guys have to be over six feet tall to cut it, so I always felt that my shorter height kept me protected in that respect. But now I'm wondering if that might be a possibility, and they staged it over by the vortex. Super soldiers are on the receiving end of mechanical implants, and they are given no choice but to kiss their prior life goodbye. They are owned by the military. In that case, eventually, there wouldn't be a shred left of the real Michael as I knew him.

"If it is the vortex, I hope they come back into the past because the present certainly isn't pretty, and Michael was gung-ho to jump with both feet into the Revolutionary War situation. I feel he's alive, but as to exactly where I have no clue. Hopefully, it's a better place than this."

"I guess waiting for word from Michael is the only option. I feel for his family with all the uncertainty," Jules said softly. Thanks for taking the risks to get the most information you did. It's hard to get a truly good answer about anything in today's world. I hope the best for him. He's such a truly nice guy."

"Friends don't come any better, for sure," Peter replied. "But there is a side of Michael that he may not have shown you. He changed in the military. He began to seek to wander onward into a hardline adventure. I have no doubt he really intended to seek out the Revolutionary War, or Civil War, whatever name you want to call it. He wanted to win or lose with both boots on. He had also heard mercenary soldiers were turning vast sums of money overseas, and he wanted to give that a whirl once the American War was over. Hearing all that last time I saw him, I started grieving over the loss of our days together. Growing up, there were small clues that questing exploration was part of his personality, but now it appears that adventure is steering his ship no matter how rough the seas get. Perhaps it has fully taken hold of him. Maybe a chance at working off of this planet could appear to him as the adventure of his dreams.

"The new version of high-risk Michael could put a woman through a lot of endless waiting and never knowing. You have to choose for yourself, but since you haven't known him for long, your exit can be less of a loss than mine is. I hope I wasn't too blunt saying that."

Jules thought for a moment. "I see your point, and no, I would have had no way to realize those things since our time together was brief. I saw no trickle of a roving spirit, but it takes time to know someone. You spared me a lot. Thanks. I couldn't take the stress of living with cycles of whether he returned or not. I'm such a metered soul."

Peter stood up. "Seems crazy, but Michael may have inadvertently given me a send-off present. Tonight, I'll deliver more loaves of bread to Brenda's friend Carrie, who lives on Amherston Street. I never would have met her without searching for information about Michael. It's funny how life goes. We just looked at one another and knew it could be for keeps. I've got to run. See you Monday." Peter offered a hand and helped Jules to her feet.

"I know Carrie! We planted together on Garden Club projects. She is special. Peter, you picked a winner. Tell her the daffodils she planted are coming up this year!" Jules said with an excited smile. "I'm so happy for you both."

"It's going to be tough on us. What with all the sneaking around to see each other. I suppose these days; you marry quickly to avoid the threat of being caught leaving your lockdown jurisdiction. One of us has to fill out a request to relocate to the other one's section of town. Oh wait, there must be a slogan for that situation. It would be, 'Your Intimate Business Is the UWN's Business'," he said with a laugh.

Jules called after him as they departed in opposite directions. "Here's my slogan for it, 'Just Do It'."

"Nick of time finding her. Carrie says that change is fast upon us, and it's of the essence that we seriously talk things over tonight. I don't want to go the next laps of life alone," Peter called back to Jules.

Jules' memories of the past had become her only comfort, besides the safety she had felt with Michael's arms around her. Jules realized that the feeling of protection in an uncertain world and Michael's rugged, handsome appeal had given her the sensation of beginning to fall in love with him. She didn't know him deeply. She was always thinking he would be back soon, and it could be sifted out then. But with new facts disclosed, living with the wear and tear of a diet of fear and separation was not a prediction for a successful relationship.

The fog was nearly thinned to nothing, and Jules had achieved sharper clarity. Although she felt a concern for Michael's well-being, Peter had never said that Michael mentioned her. By that token, and the fact that they only briefly dated, she actually could not lay claim to any relationship with Michael at all, just friendship. What Peter had told her made sense. Michael did share his thoughts about his future with Peter. He did not hint at any future with her. The heavy amount of time Michael spent with her while on leave meant he subtracted that time from what he would have spent with Peter or his mother and sister. It was totally possible he had been already in the process of separating himself from his past. Although they had spent the vast majority of his leave together, Michael had not pressured her into sleeping with him or creating ties that bind. They had simply enjoyed being together and discussed the past but made no reach for a future in their conversation.

Peter was bearing the heavier loss. Michael had been his lifelong friend. Jules felt thankful that Carrie had opened the door of possibility between herself and Peter. Everyone has every right to be themselves, even if their chosen path leads to unfortunate and unexpected events. Michael had left his best friend Peter, his mother, his sister, and her hanging on the edge to follow his dreams. He had every right to listen to his own heart and seek to find his own destiny. One thing Jules was sure of is that a happy relationship can't be built upon either party's unhappiness. Michael wasn't looking for a home and hearth. Michael would likely end up with adventure and then any port in a storm. Happiness is in the eye of the beholder. One size does not fit all.

One piece of Peter's information solidly stood out. If Michael had been hell-bent on fighting for old America, then the Revolutionary War would still be ongoing and very real. Those in the military would know if that war was still going on. It was hard to envision winning against the government with its nasty medley of ultimate weapons, but the love of a country can accomplish amazing things. Maybe with more extended patience, a haven from today's reality might emerge.

Jules turned the corner onto her street, only to face the clamor of two of the substantial-sized residential homes being emptied out by town employees. Usually, cleanouts were completed in the wee hours of the morning, but these two homes seemed like rush jobs. The residents had been couples of professional, educated status. Jules' heart sank. Her journal documented her suspicion that the removal of the elderly from their homes would progress to the next step, which would be to include the well-educated. Another of her fears appeared to be coming to fruition.

More Newcomers of who knows what kind would be placed into her neighborhood. The size of each home would likely hold at least 15 new residents per each. A nagging question re-emerged. If the homeowners were just relocating, why wouldn't they take their possessions? The town was only going to confiscate what was left behind, sell the things as used, and keep the money made. Wouldn't the prior residents need at least some of their basic personal items?

CHAPTER THREE

Any trace of the fog had now dissipated completely. Jules sighed as she tied up her hair, tossed a tattered blue tarp on the ground, and slipped on the pair of her father's frayed, thick leather gloves. She whispered under her breath, "Dad, Mom, I'm so grateful that you both lived your full lives, never seeing what was to become of the country you both loved so much." Jules stretched, swayed several times back and forth to loosen up, and then began rhythmically raking the leaves off of her lawn. She appreciated that the rain had stopped, and only a gentle breeze fanned the air. It would make her task a lot easier.

During her father's lifetime, he had persisted in saving items long past their usefulness or just in case he needed to remove parts from the item to repair something else in a creative manner. The household rule was that no repair parts were ever purchased until her father first checked what he had in his garage. The garage remained as a museum and a testament to his ingenuity. The contents of his garage had been the source of family humor, but now she was grateful for every item he had left behind, especially his favorite work-battered gloves. The sight of them on his old workbench always stirred welcome memories for Jules. Even though the size of the gloves slowed her efforts, using them seemed her best option to curtail the persistent rash barehanded exposure to the synthetic leaves had caused her.

Rain or shine, Jules, like all residents, was expected to have a perfectly cleared lawn by inspection time. Her father had taught her early on to cheerfully go about whatever the task at hand was. It has proven an excellent attribute to foster in times such as these. "Thanks, Dad," she thought with a quick smile. Jules could not help but wish that when she completed the raking, one of her mom's warm suppers would be waiting just like it used to be. Now, her mother's apple pie was only served in dreams.

Things worked out best for Jules if she delayed supper and began the task right after the walk home from work. Two-plus years ago, the local government abruptly removed all residential front yard trees. In their stead, they planted twelve-foot, vile, synthetic, fast-growing bio-engineered trees. During the raking, the smell of the leaves permeated her clothes so intensely that she was forced to change into fresh clothes in the garage before entering the house.

For a moment, Jules paused, leaned on her rake, surveyed the volume of downed leaves, shook her head, and then let her thoughts drift back to better times. She remembered the spreading, crimson maple trees that had graced her yard in previous years. The traditional leaf raking in the fall had been profuse, but the maples had held their leaves perfectly through the spring and summer months. Whether bare of their leaves and creating impressive silhouettes against the winter snow, graciously shading the yard from the summer heat, or budding forth with the promise of another spring, they had perfectly complemented their red brick pre-Civil War historic home. Her parents had planted the two crimson maples the year she was born. Those maple trees had stood as centennials for thirty years. They had stretched their branches as they grew and contributed uniquely to each passing season.

With eyes closed, Jules paused and visualized being five when her father introduced her to the voice of those maples. In spring, the leaves had a soft whispering sound, while during summer, they had a full-bodied, louder, swooshing tone. By fall, the sound of the leaves developed a rasp that increased until they dried enough to tumble to the ground. The wind made the leaves talk and sometimes chatter among one another. Her childish diving into a crisp pile of maple leaves had never failed to deliver a rewarding woodland aroma and bring a warm expression upon her father's face.

A Native American Proverb was still hanging over his old workbench. She remembered him bringing that sign home from a trip to a local flea market.

Listen to the Wind. It Talks.

Listen to the Silence. It Speaks.

Listen to Your Heart. It Knows.

Since Jules turned thirty, she had begun to listen to her heart. Working as a teacher to small children established a certain clarity within her. Just as she had verged upon the realization that she longed for a special relationship and children of her own, the world as she had known it had taken on an ugly twist. Despite the troubled times, she had made up her mind to give Michael a chance, but her heart didn't immediately answer. Now, her heart had given her a firm response: no, for the happiness of all concerned.

Jules' mind turned back to the work at hand. She would have to write up her journal tonight, as she did every Friday, to document her thoughts on the Friday class information. If she analyzed the situation, she could suppose what was next and try to be prepared for it. She might as well toss in the dishtowel, so to speak, since her thoughts were going to be on a negative train ride tonight while writing in her journal. She could try to fill Saturday with thoughts of a nicer vein.

The synthetic trees that the government had developed were an assault on the eye. They appeared distinctly artificial, failing to imitate the artful hand of the nature Jules dearly loved. Thick, rubbery, barked trunks supported an ugly and disproportionate branch structure. The large, yellow, sticky, sickly-looking leaves had such an accelerated life cycle that the trees shed some of their leaves daily. From the drip line to the trunk, the earth had become toxic under the canopies of the genetic creations. The town mowed the lawns every third week of the month unless the homeowner opted to mow their lawn, which Jules elected to do because it was necessary in order to rake the leaves at a better pace.

Jules treated her leaf collection as a priority no matter how hard the wind blew or how late her supper became. Jules vowed that the last thing she intended to do was give up the home she had lived in since birth. She could feel a bitter edge mounting inside her that she had to conceal at all costs.

The rubbery synthetic leaves released a distinctively unpleasant, diesel fuel-type odor that had come to dominate the air during the generic sameness of every season. Daily raking of the leaves only added another layer of the heavy, lingering, depressing stench. Gone were the ordinary joys of sitting on the porch or opening windows to air the house. The intermittent laughter of neighborhood children at outdoor play had fallen silent. That silence implied a diminished New Amerikan future.

Jules continued raking the thick and disgustingly oily-smelling leaves from the bio-trees. The taller and wider the trees grew, the larger the circle of dead, poisoned grass around them became. The environmental improvement program had only led to further restrictions being forced upon the residents. 'Your Guide to Residential Living' regulation manuals were issued to all homeowners. The section concerning the bio-trees stated that it was mandatory that all residents participate in the daily harvest of any fallen synthetic leaves. Each day, the leaves were to be placed in the leaf recycling bins provided to each property owner. The maximum penalty for failing to comply with the leaf collection was losing the right to live independently in a private residence and being relegated to reside elsewhere. It was the government's way of blamelessly stealing the assets of the general public. The results of any non-compliance always included words like somewhere or elsewhere.

Initially, the 'Daily Leaf Harvest Law' did not concern Jules. She had been used to raking her massive maple leaves in the fall. Jules had supposed that raking would be unnecessary during the winter season. Buffalo, New York, traditionally had snowfall, but she had been proven wrong. Weather manipulation was firmly entrenched now. Global warming was blamed for the extreme daily temperatures. For the past several years, the winter season had only yielded rain every early afternoon for several hours, and that equated to year-round daily raking. The only trace of the four seasons that continued to exist was the sunrise and sunset location, and that clue was diminished by artificial cloud cover.

In the initial phases of the environmental project, the old or infirm neighbors who could not comply were promptly ordered to vacate their property, and the government relocated those residents. The homes swiftly became the government's property. That's when Jules first noticed that the prior residents appeared to have left all their possessions completely behind. The vacant houses had their bio-trees harvested for wood. The trees were replaced with new bio trees during the next planting season after the home was reoccupied. The town government always had a profusion of confiscated used items for sale to other residents at inflated prices. All stores that sold new items had closed one after another.

During the last two-plus years, Jules quietly noticed the ongoing changes made to her neighborhood. The government seeded what they referred to as Newcomers into being occupants of the empty houses. The Newcomers appeared to be from foreign countries, and Jules suspected the replacement residents to be those who were likely recent border crossers judging by their gang member tattoos and furtive looks. Usually, multiple men were assigned to each house. So far, Jules had seen no families with children when everyone was raking their yards. A couple, known as the Shrivers, had moved into a government-owned house two doors down from her. They lurked by their windows but never trod outdoors, or so her casual older friend Miriam, who lived next door, had mentioned. They didn't have their bio-trees, or "stink and rakes," as the guys at work called them, replanted in their front yard as yet. So far, Jules had never gotten a chance to get a clear look at them.

Jules knew that the Regulation Police, fully dressed in protective wear, complete with respirators, would appear like clockwork every evening to weigh and empty each household's leaf recycling bin and inspect the exterior of each residence. Fines were issued for any bio-leaves on the ground upon their arrival or anything out of place in the front yards. Any parked automobiles had to be kept spotless. The aggressive patrol excluded the backyards from their daily scrutiny. They weren't eager to confront the random looters who roamed the neighborhoods and considered all backyards their private turf.

The leaf collection reports were given to the town to allow them to distribute allotments for heat, water, and electric use to law-abiding residents. Back when her maple trees were removed, Jules had expressed her disgust over the replacement trees. Instead of leaving her yard with two bio-trees, they returned and planted a third one. Lesson learned. It surely caused additional leaves to rake, but it also gave her a higher credit allowance for electricity and water, which in turn yielded excess to use for growing some vegetables and highlights to her week, which was her being able to indulge in wonderful hot baths.

Burning any synthetic branches was strictly forbidden. Any burning of such caused a thick, odorous, black smoke that clung to the window glass, screening, and siding of any buildings in the vicinity of those fires. The towns pruned the synthetic trees and turned the branches over to the government. Jules had heard that the branches were processed into industrial-use pellets in exchange for additional fuel credits for the town proper.

So far, Jules remained dutiful and grateful that she was treated as a law-abiding resident when allotted her utility allowance. Jules continued to bend into the task at hand, her resilience shining through. The daily wind was always an unpredictable factor, but she was fairly early on the collection list. As the time for leaf collection neared, she would quickly double-check her lawn for any newly fallen leaves that had drifted down just before the Regulation Police arrived.

CHAPTER FOUR

Jules continued raking and steeped herself in past memories, recalling how the prior two years had transpired.

At first, Jules had suspected that leaf raking was part of the government's 'War Against Obesity' campaign, perhaps another way to promote regular exercise. After several years under the yoke of daily raking, she realized that it was likely just another way of declaring citizens unable to live independently. The law proved to be a perfect scheme that legitimatized the government confiscation of the personal assets of its citizens. 'You Rake or We Take' clearly summed up the situation at hand. This year, the slogan was boldly printed on the citations handed out and on the collection trucks.

Jule's thoughts drifted. She badly wanted to brush an errant strand of hair away from her eyes, but the thought of getting the odor on her hair prohibited any such action. She vowed that despite the deluge of daily propaganda, she would keep the facts straight. The American way of life had suffered a number of radical adjustments with the onset of the government's demands upon its citizens. It was mandatory that citizens work only to achieve collective, appropriate thinking and achievements, and personal goals had to be abandoned. 'Freedom Promotes Terrorism' became one of the UWN's billboard slogans. Jules tried to stifle the anger that flickered within her. No matter how many people had voted to preserve their rights, when the votes were counted, rights had dwindled away, one after another. Jules noticed yet another sharp pain in her temple. She suspected a full-blown headache was looming within the hour.

New pressures never seemed to cease. Any town with a high personal violation rate was subject to semi-annual penalties, and severe ramifications were suffered for at least six months. Once a municipality was cited for noncompliance, it was subject to discriminatory weather changes and lower utility, including water allotments. Random local food shortages that reached crisis proportions were created. Regulations and doling out the necessities had become the norm, but in the case of a town in violation, all allotments were further rationed.

Jules' town had already experienced a town-wide penalty early on in the program. Neighborhood violence flourished against those who had caused the sanction. No police protection was provided to citizens concerning disturbances. The government advocated that reporting any possible violations was the best way to cleanse a town from within. That yielded neighbor against neighbor, friend against friend, and many families ceased communication out of fear of malicious trumped-up charges. Emotionally isolating citizens was a tool that the government had honed to perfection.

Jules felt another pulsing pain in her temple. She realized that she had forgotten to remove her headband. In appreciation for one's employment, it was suggested that citizens proudly and constantly wear their headbands, which were emblazoned with the logo of an individual's government employer. It occurred to Jules that she seemed more susceptible to headaches when wearing hers. She usually took it off as soon as she returned home. Liberating a rebellious surge within her, she ripped her headband off and tossed it toward her porch.

It had quickly become a futile effort to plant a vegetable garden with fluctuating water restrictions in place, the soil quality deteriorating, not to mention backyard looters. At first, the government had further regulated any planting with lengthy applications and expensive permits. That curtailed outdoor gardening a year ago, but it stood to reason that backyard gardening and personal yard use would cease when the fear of the gangs roaming the neighborhood and rummaging in yards severely increased. It was worse than when an occasional bear would focus on the yards and create fear and havoc. Recently, any possible permit excluded home vegetable gardens because growing food on personally owned property was declared illegal.

Jules stood and rested a moment before dragging the tarp closer to her depository box by the road. Her stomach turned as she became further engulfed in waves of the offensive, greasy smell from the leaves. Even the weeds, which she called a lawn, had turned gray where leaves had fallen and stayed on the ground through the afternoon rainfall. Her eyes felt irritated. She gave the rest of her front yard a cursory glance for any item out of place. With the exception of her car, she found that all seemed to be in order.

"Sorry, Mom and Dad," she whispered under her breath. "For a moment, let me be honest. This situation is truly a bitch. Honestly, I am not cheerful about doing this night after night, but I promise that I will. I know that I have to. The only life I will have had is what we all shared here. The only comfort I can reach for is here, where my memories reside."

CHAPTER FIVE

Cars had become useless items to own. No one was allotted a chance to use them. Even public transportation was no longer available. No one in the working class had enough money to buy or operate a car if they wanted to. Yet citizens owning autos were expected to keep them polished and dirt-free in their driveways or receive a fine. Before her supper, she would have to run a dry cloth over her bumpers and maybe the interior. It would seem simpler to park a car in the garage and leave it there, but it was illegal to conceal automotive assets. Life had developed into a series of endless rules.

The back of Jule's neck began to itch, but at least with her headband off, there was no further sharp discipline that she had begun to suspect was a result of her non-condoned private thoughts. Once she had realized the work shirt of her uniform was causing a rash, she began wearing an old cotton shirt underneath it. The uniforms were always laundered at work. She assumed that it was either their detergent or the contents of the fabric. Although she had been allergy-free for years, she had always had sensitive skin as a child. There was a chance she was currently developing an allergy. If anyone noticed her rash at work, it would cause her immediate departure to a Midwest clinic. The 'Laws for the Common Good' required that citizens turn themselves over for testing at the first sign of any illness. No one was anxious to try that law on for size, so everyone concealed everything wrong and silently limped along until their health improved or death provided an exit.

All the remaining independent farms had been confiscated by the government. Barns were used as centers for clinical testing and as locations where the elderly were put out to pasture at the first signs of illness. Jules suspected the elderly did not graze there for any lengthy period, just long enough for their families to develop an out-of-sight, out-of-mind attitude. She would have investigated her suspicions a few years ago, but now the government had become too powerful for anyone to risk seeking the truth. In days gone by, she would have blogged away about any infringement she noticed. Jules mused and whispered, "Were these places the location of the infamous unnamed elsewhere?"

Eradicating chronic diseases was a special interest government program. Jules was of the unspoken opinion that the reduction of chronic disease in America had everything to do with a low survival rate of sick individuals. The new government anticipated the ideal lifespan for citizens was to be sixty-two years of age.

She thought it ironic that Americans used to celebrate their independence gained on July 4. During the last year, seventy-six had become a physical age that was nearly impossible to obtain. July 4 had become a holiday when the government celebrated those who had voluntarily come forward and opted to have their lives terminated on July 4. It was always, always, for the common good.

Jules kept systematically raking the lawn. She thought about the downward spiral that everyday life had experienced over the last two years. The pharmacies were now operating as government walk-in clinics. Even nonprescription medicines were doled out. Any indication of illness now required a full investigative report. Jules had dried herbs and had them tucked away rather than face scrutiny at the pharmacy. She tried to push away her concerns. Her early childhood allergies had generally been only food-related. Jules shuttered, realizing she could not control what her future held. Hopes and dreams had grown out of reach. Whatever would happen to her would simply be a cruel twist of fate.

During the workday, Jules steeled her mind into silent acceptance. Being with her friends on the team created a pleasant diversion. The government managed to make the future bleaker with each passing month, and regulations only got further out of control. She used to write about injustice on the Internet before free speech was silenced, and to the general public, the web was now unreachable. All she wrote now were entries in her journal, where her anger increasingly seeped through.

She took a break from harvesting the leaves and switched her attention to her black cherry Chevy Tahoe. She slipped the key in the ignition every month and turned it over. When she heard the engine rumble to life, the familiar sound seemed to revive her strength. She glanced at the fuel gauge. It registered half a tank of gasoline. She periodically used some of her lawn mower gas for her car. The leaves had killed half of her lawn, and the car had to be moved to keep the tires in good stead.

With each periodic start, Jules was overwhelmed with the desire to back down the driveway and cruise off into the unknown. She backed the Tahoe to the end of her driveway, gunned the motor, and drove with the sunroof open up to her garage. Then, with a sigh, she backed the car back into its usual parking spot. One of Michael's favorite comments drifted through her mind, 'No guts, no glory'. Jules rolled down the driver's side window and closed her eyes. The breeze swept her face, however, it was tainted with the pungent smell of the leaves. If she could muster the guts to seek the glory maybe there still were possibilities out there in the somewhere.

The immediate block of the street was quiet, bare of any signs of any existence. Jules heart rate tapped an increased rhythm as she considered taking her only chance at escape. No one in the neighborhood had tried to simply drive away. Perhaps it was possible to accomplish the unexpected. With the driver-side window rolled down and the sunroof open, the fresh breeze would caress her face. For the last time, she would back down the driveway and drive on, relishing the sweet taste of freedom until the engine stumbled and the gas tank had spoken its final drop and declared itself empty. Sometimes, she dreamed she could hear the tires on the pavement beneath her and that only a few miles away, beyond her town's limits, America had won the Revolutionary War and now existed just the way it had in the past. For a week or more after pondering those thoughts, she found herself with a gnawing hunger for what used to be ordinary days, and it was difficult for her to recalibrate into the new reality.

Jules issued a sigh of shame. Finding herself at a loss for the guts to proceed, she turned the key, and the engine ceased its spark of life. With only four thousand miles on the odometer, the interior still maintained the faint smell of freedom of choice. At the current rate of non-usage, she wagered her four-wheel drive, without oil changes needed, would outlive her. Jules had always nicknamed her cars, but this shining beauty had to sit in her driveway like a useless hunk of fated plastic and metal. The only name she could think to give it was Road's End, but that would be admitting her life was stripped of possibilities and would be terminal soon, too.

Providing there were no neighborhood disturbances, she looked forward to a quiet day of Saturday household chores. On Friday nights, she usually updated her personal journal concerning political changes that were laid out during the educational classes. Writing her journal gave her a chance to express her true sentiments privately and shed some bitter tears. Living alone, Jules could afford moments of raw emotion. She always finalized her entry by projecting any new grief that she thought the government held up its sleeve, waiting and ready to become the next stranglehold exacted upon the citizens.

Several areas were emphatically stressed during today's classes. Jules had learned to sit and absorb the information and wait to analyze it later. It was the only way she could manage to attend the training without acquiring a screaming headache. She finished cleaning up the Chevy's exterior while she mentally worked through the material presented during today's class.

The instructor mentioned, "Citizens are planned to be relocated according to trade aptitudes. The new compound communities are designed to be off-limits to nonresidents while society is being restructured as a positive step toward reducing the upsurge of violent crimes. Not only will relocation offer the convenience of citizens living where they can best serve their government, but the new walled-in compounds will be monitored closer by resident government agents. These model high-rise communities will better provide the residents with protection from the constant violence that has been sweeping neighborhoods. All transferees are required to leave the majority of their property and possessions behind for government liquidation. The new community residents will all be allowed equal transfer credit value to ensure a redistribution of wealth, which remains one of the government's primary goals."

Jules felt positive that the relocation to a compound was a design to accelerate the ripping off of the principal assets of anyone selected to be transferred. It seemed crystal clear to Jules that those who crossed the line and inflicted violence ought to be the ones up for some sort of relocation. Jules summed things up in her head. Since neighborhood and domestic violence were left unchecked, the government appeared to be using the situation to make people willing to be relocated and walled into compounds out of fear for their own safety. Jules wondered what would happen if spouses had diverse trade aptitudes. She doubted that AI would care since emotional relationships were beyond its comprehension.

Jules didn't worry about the possibility of being selected for relocation. She was already reduced to the lowest status, that of a government factory worker. Jules reasoned that factory jobs were temporary until total robotic use was implemented. Then, the workers would go somewhere. Until then, they would likely leave her embedded with the rabble and hope she and those like her got taken out.

Jules suspected that she had been stripped of her teaching credentials not only for her questioning of education's new objectives but also because of the cautionary articles she had written during the period of change before the United World Nation took directional control of every country around the globe. She had dared to question the motives of the previous American government's sell-out of their citizen's rights and the exhaustion of moral leadership. She would be forever enshrined on the government's watch list of potential homeland terrorists, but with a side note that she had been a congenial and productive factory worker, she had raked the leaves well, but in her case, too much education had sealed her fate.

Crime was up, and arrests were down. Criminals had guns. The average citizen had only household items or good old-fashioned pitchforks and shovels that they could use to defend themselves. A scene from an old Frankenstein movie flashed through her mind.

For the last five years, Jules had faithfully kept her journal up to date with whatever information she heard and her future predictions. Her bleakest suppositions kept ringing true. Immediately after the removal of remaining citizen rights, there had been a period of such dissent that most of the ammunition anyone had was either discharged or stolen. Jules was surprised that the government did not confiscate weapons from the citizens, but as things transpired, she realized the government wanted the confrontation in order to eliminate the worst opposition early in their game plan. Within a relatively short period, guns became useless without the right size cartridges. Jules still had the same five cartridges that her father had left behind.

During the first year of the formation of the United World Nation, bands of veteran soldiers, re-enactors, and ranchers operated as tossed-together revolutionary units. Gunfire in the hill areas was frequently heard. Many teenage boys had indoctrinated themselves deeply into a warlike frame of mind by years of intense use of military video games. They slipped away after nightfall, joining up as Freedom Fighters, only to meet head-on with the actual reality of death.

Drones were used to surveil neighborhoods where any extension of hope and encouragement was suspected of being harbored by the revolutionaries. The government tagged any unaccounted-for citizen as a homeland terrorist. Revolutionaries were driven into the woodland hills and national parks. The government then set massive fires in order to eliminate any places of refuge for the Freedom Fighters.

Many citizens walked with their heads down and avoided eye contact. But hope kindled deep in the eyes of the majority as long as conflict could be heard in the distance. Rumors had spread that the battle still continued, especially in some states further west of the Mississippi River and in the Deep South. The government reduced the news to brief television coverage about new regulations. Time passed as the pages of her journal turned. Cut off and continually isolated from information, ordinary citizens quickly became more concerned with their daily lives and the dutiful compliance inflicted on them. There was no publicly touted victory over the revolution, but by the government's conduct towards the ordinary citizen, it was clearly understood who was in the driver's seat. If there was a haven left on earth, the citizens were immobilized to seek it out.

CHAPTER SIX

The majority of a week's salary was deducted and then co-mingled in a government-managed account. Per government literature, most of what was withheld from wages was used to maintain an individual from retirement age to the end of their calculated lifespan. Jules wondered if anyone else had noticed that despite a substantial pay deduction, the retirement age of a worker was sixty-two, and the life expectancy age was precisely the same number of years. Retirement savings were likely yet another looming rip-off.

A paltry weekly difference was issued as personal cash. In order to use any part of that cash for a miscellaneous purchase, one had to beg a Government Dispersal Clerk and convince them it was a needed item. Recycled items the government had confiscated from others were used to fulfill the common citizen's requests for merchandise. Jules had quickly learned to tape everything that broke or live without it. She kept her father's rolls of duct tape in a climate-controlled temperature as well as she could. It had to last her. Jules even had a roll of twenty-four-inch wide duct tape in case a window broke or she needed to barter.

The old edge of her anger over the incident where she had gotten burned by being allotted and paying for a toaster that didn't even operate reawakened within her. Jules realized the priciest items were clearly black market. After her sandals went missing from her front porch step, Jules had found them in the Town inventory for sale at twice the price they had been when she bought them new. When she needed thirty-dollar shoes, she asked for ones worth forty, knowing they would cut her back to a thirty-dollar allotment value. Government Dispersal Clerks thought of themselves as small gods who worked for a commission for any savings they could verify by reducing outgoing allotment requests. Worst of all, common citizens had to accept the fact that the dispersal worker's commission also had to be paid directly to them in cash at the time of the transaction. Common thieves were pikers when compared to the government's treatment of its citizens and their assets.

Jules glanced up after she finished rubbing down the Tahoe. The sky was loaded with crisscross striping created by the climate control drones. After years of weather control, it was no small wonder why only the new synthetic plants could thrive. She closed her eyes and pictured the brilliant blue skies that were part and parcel of her mother's old, printed calendars featuring bountiful rural America. On Friday nights, she always found her thoughts drifting. She used half of the one day off of work to discipline her mindset and blank out her thoughts before approaching the coming work week. She decided she would be better off savoring memories of the true American past during her supper. Her little table sat where her mother's calendar pictures hung ceiling-high upon the basement wall. She returned to the drudgery of harvesting the leaves and evaluating her class instruction material.

It was today's second topic that concerned Jules the most. The 'War Against Obesity' was now moving to the plateau of a full-force assault. The appropriate weight for height clauses wouldn't harshly affect her. At a height of five foot five and weighing one hundred ten pounds, she was within the guidelines. It was not the result of extra exercise. She simply had meager food choices due to all the additives. Jules had gotten into the habit of eating very little. She mentally reviewed the rest of the day's government study session in order to prepare to write journal notes after supper.

The instructor's words had fallen heavily upon the workers, "Voluntary weight reduction has failed throughout the United World Nation. Obesity continues to strain the world system. By the end of the coming week, every citizen will be assigned an ideal weight based on their height, bone structure, and occupation. An individual chart showing weekly expected weight loss, beginning two weeks thereafter and over the next six months, will be provided to every citizen, both adult and child. Weekly weigh-ins will be accomplished at your place of employment, at the schools, or convenient government weigh scales located at your Town Hall. The official slogan is 'Shape up in Six'.

"At the end of next week, grocery items will no longer be available for purchase by the average citizen. Food will now be rationed and shipped to each individual household based on age and the number of citizens, using the currently provided resident census taken by the town officials. Government-recommended caloric intake charts will be custom-tailored for each citizen. Non-cooperation with the government weight loss and maintenance program will result in reductions in wages and employment dismissal for repeat offenders. Parental failure to reduce the weight of their children according to the plan will result in the removal of children by the end of the six-month period."

Jules sensed that this was another tactic that was part and parcel of achieving their goal of world population reduction. Due to the slanted administration of health care, those with chronic diseases had not been able to obtain the care they needed on a timely basis. Jules suspected that no dietary concessions were slated for those with specialty illnesses because the issue was not addressed. Changing the diets of children was bound to cause dissension within households.

Ignorantly, the children would beg to be removed and placed into institutional care. It would be far easier to eliminate the parents once they were separated from their children rather than forcefully dismembering families. As proven in the past, every government order held embedded multiple prongs of attack.

The theft had actually reduced itself in the last year. No one wanted appliances that burned energy they did not have to spare. There was no black market for electronic items, but now real food would become high in demand. Most people had some canned goods on hand. They would be forced to do battle to retain them. The new game called Hunger would bring about fighting in the streets over scraps of food in order to fill their voids. Cooking whatever scarce remaining rabbits, rats, possums, or woodchucks looked like a possible prediction.

Jules had been careful to avoid any kind of food that might cause her to have a food allergy. She was deathly afraid to be labeled as chronically ill. She had specifically avoided the prevalent offerings of genetically altered food. Her acceptable variety of food had dwindled down to a meager list. Once her outdoor vegetable gardening became illegal, she turned to relying on the freeze-dried supplies that she had purchased before the UWN government took over and what she could grow indoors. She would have no way of knowing the actual ingredients embedded in the government-issued food. She had enough real dehydrated food left for another six-month period. Hoarding food could automatically declare anyone a terrorist. At the moment, she could only guess what would happen if the government extended the program, which they were always prone to do. Jules had enough stored food to take her beyond this year's upcoming July 4 date.

Jules struggled to control the thoughts that worried her. She realized she was emotionally better off facing each day as it came rather than dreaming she could escape to freedom. She would likely end up in what they called the elsewhere. She would never be removed from the watch list, and her number would be up sooner or later. Eventually, she would be erased off the face of the earth, along with millions more of the earth's undesirable inhabitants. She suspected that the lists, comprised of millions of people to be eradicated to dust, were made three years ago. She had no way to fathom what the current world population exactly was at the moment. She trusted that some government computer somewhere was devoted to tabulating that statistic. Void of any consideration, in some darkened warehouse, AI was likely creating termination forecasts, effects, and rosters for the next round of elimination.

Jules choked back her tears. There was simply no chance for her to look forward to a life that was more than what her everyday life had been reduced to. In fact, things would only close in tighter until her choking point was reached. Her week spent with Michael had awakened her dream of a full, normal life, but now, even that chance had managed to fall flat. There was no love of a lifetime ahead, no child of her own in the future, no returning to teaching in a classroom, and certainly, no additional freedom to be found under any stone left on what had once been God's green earth because all now belonged to the United World Nation. It was the middle of March, and in a few more months there would be the open annual invitation day of July 4. She could ask for anything for a last meal and then quietly go into the long, good night.

Jules paused her raking and slapped her own face for considering such a thing, but there, for a moment, in her mind's eye, she knew she would ask for six fresh frosted jelly-filled donuts and a large coffee from a Tim Hortons store. In the first year of the UWN, Tim Hortons Café and Bake Shop had been tossed into oblivion along with the sport called Hockey. If they couldn't produce those particular donuts, she could decline termination, which she knew in her heart was foolish to even consider, and tell them better luck next time. Somehow, the free-wheeling downslide of everything changing constantly had to cease, but the United World Nation's only offer was a voluntary termination held annually on July 4.

CHAPTER SEVEN

It was almost 3 PM. Jules made up her mind to wait until after the Youth Cadet Patrol had passed her house before she put her garbage bin on the street. She disliked the brazen attitude they had and the way they pawed through your trash right in front of you. The Youth Cadet Patrol was more than eager to get people in the neighborhood into trouble. If you even dared address them, they tried to write a citation. Depending upon the number of tickets they wrote, the cadets earned points to obtain chances at the 'Vacation of a Lifetime Lottery' and other rewards. They preyed on anyone over fifty as much as they could manage because those tickets yielded them extra bonus points.

Life had certainly sunk to a bottom rung when immature children with the worst attitudes had become instrumental in sealing your fate. She often wondered what level of indoctrination had been put in place at the schools since she left her profession. It had become such a common occurrence for children to turn against their parents and neighbors.

The Youth Patrol Cadet who gave Jules the worst shiver was definitely Zandell Trell. He was a short, bow-legged, slump-shouldered, overweight ten-year-old who was the self-appointed leader of the local pack. His face always bore witness to glasses clouded with filth, as well as contempt, and the remnants of the last trash food he devoured. The buttons on his cadet shirt strained to cover the rolls of his excess fat. Every night, he could be seen strutting down the street, jamming his face with remnants he gleaned out of trash cans, and wiping his face on his sleeve to partially remove the traces of food and wipe his unceasingly crusted runny nose.

Jules was willing to wager that the new diet was only going to make him meaner as he got leaner. She doubted if there would even be any spare scraps of food in people's trash for the cadets to feast on. Jules expected the Youth Cadets would eventually start coming door to door demanding food despite the fact that they, too, were expected to achieve weight loss. Leaving a cadet sweets in your trash was a method of avoiding citations, but Jules refused to participate in the now-established custom.

Jules noticed a neighborhood teenager with his huge dog meticulously checking the exterior of the mailboxes. He generally walked his dog before the Youth Cadet Patrol began their rounds. The fact that he was able to afford to feed a dog, let alone one that size, made Jules feel suspicious of him. All mail was pre-read at the Postal Exchange before delivery. His attention to the mailboxes made little, if any, sense. As he drew closer, Jules noticed that it appeared that he was using a pocket knife to scrape color-coded stickers off of the mailboxes. Everyone knew that all the streetlights had cameras on them that recorded daily activity. Jules wondered how he could behave so boldly unless he were in league with the government, but she kept her head down and minded her own business when he busied himself with her mailbox.

Society had managed to groom everyone to suspect everybody else. New friendships were dangerous to pursue, and old ones were now uncertain. People had begun turning one another in for even suspected activity. It all seemed based on the unlikely belief that the restrictions would ease once the area troublemakers were apprehended.

Jules decided she'd better reduce the weight of the tarp and then finish raking the remainder of the leaves. When she turned to pull the tarp up to the recycle bin, she realized that the teen was standing on her lawn behind her.

"I have time to give you a hand, Miss Jules," he said in a rather timid manner. "That is, if you'll allow me to. I'm Gabe from just down the street. Here's the mail from your mailbox. You are right outside, so I thought I would save you the time you'd need to check for your mail."

The boy's headband reflected attendance at the School of United World Nation, level eleven. The boy appeared older than sixteen. Even if she discounted his near six-foot height, there was a captivating sense of maturity that lay in his warm brown eyes. He offered her a straight-on look with no shades of deception. It was a rarity to find anyone who would dare to catch and hold another's glance. A slight breeze picked up, and more leaves tumbled to the ground. She had a rock-hard headache from the smell of the leaves.

"I'd love some help, but you know the rules. You can't help anyone older than yourself," Jules answered.

"It's not a problem. I can handle the Youth Cadets. They're afraid of my dog. I'm a quick worker, and in the worst-case scenario, I can seem older than you," he replied. "Watch this," Gabe said as he turned his back to her. When he turned back around, his facial features appeared to be changed, and he looked close to fifty. He even provided a convincing slight slump to his shoulders.

"How did you do that?" Jules asked with amazement.

"Dad and I spent some time in California. I did well in acting school because I have what they called a flexible face," Gabe said as he laughed himself back to normal.

Based on the edge of sincerity in his eyes and more than a twinge of curiosity, Jules suddenly pushed aside her conservative judgment and suspicion. In that instant, she listened to her dangerous beat of the heart and opted to accept his assistance.

"Put my mail on the porch, and I'll go and get a second rake," Jules replied as she hurried into the garage.

Jules handed Gabe a rake. "At work, they call this little duty the stink and rake."

"They sure called that one right," Gabe said as he took the rake from her hand and then proceeded on to smack the trunks of all three trees. More leaves fluttered to the ground. "Great name for the task. Might as well make tomorrow's job easier for you," he said with a pleasant smile.

As they began raking, Jules noticed that Gabe had an extremely efficient way of raking the leaves and moving the tarp as he progressed. She began using the same strokes after realizing the job could be buttoned up sooner if she mirrored his method.

"There you go. We make an excellent duo when raking," Gabe remarked.

Jules ventured a neutral comment, "Your dog is exceptionally large. Is he an Irish Wolfhound? He has the size and trademark golden eyes."

"You're right. He's an Irish Wolfhound with a mix of something else, which gives him a heavy load of fortitude. Bill Whitacre trained him, and they still have sessions together now and again. Nemo's well-behaved, and he'll watch and wait on the lawn until I'm done helping you," Gabe explained. He paused and then continued, "Today is garbage day, but you have nothing to fear from the Youth Cadet Patrol when my Captain Nemo is in your yard and on duty.

My dog is bigger than most of the kids who aim to cause trouble. They're quite afraid of him because he's one-hundred-eighty pounds, thirty-four inches at the shoulder, and seven feet tall standing up on his hind legs. He can lick clean a kitchen counter just casually standing on all fours, but my dad is disappointed because he holds his huge tail in a downward position so he can't dust the coffee table. Oh well, no one ever promised life would be perfect."

The dog took a friendly attitude as he scrutinized Jules. The dog seemed to sense Gabe was bragging about him. Nemo began to growl under his breath when Zandell Trell, with his arrogant strut of authority, began approaching. Zandrell was clearly acting out his self-proclaimed role, and the dog was clearly critical of the Cadet.

Zandell yelled over to Gabe, "Hey, Dumb-oh. Are you practicing up for work camp? I could write you up for helping someone older than you."

"Move along, Troll. I'm allowed to help her because she's going to be my new mother," Gabe boldly called back.

"Well now, ain't she just dumber than she looks," Zandell retorted. "She better not let that dog of yours do his business in her front yard if she knows what's good for her. I'm itching to write her a citation." Zandell gave Gabe an ugly sneer and moved on to the neighbor's garbage can, where he paused, nosily and noisily, and began a clatter while searching around in their trash.

Gabe waited until Zandell was out of earshot. "I saw him slip two plastic milk jugs into your front ivy last night. I'll get them in your trash and turn the can out to the street. He'll be sour grapes upon his return here. He's sure you didn't find the milk jugs and thinks that he can write you up a citation. He's got some nerve, especially since you are a revered memory as a teacher at school. I hear mentions about you. The kids refer to you as the 'Teacher of the Talking Flowers'."

Jules was surprised, "They still remember the Mother's Day projects?"

"They sure do. Last week, someone even wrote with chalk on the sidewalk: 'Bring Back the Teacher of the Talking Flowers'," Gabe answered. "You are a legend."

"I miss the kids too, " Jules said with a sigh. When their eyes locked, Jules asked, "Why on earth did you blurt out to Zandrell that I intended on becoming your new mother?"

Gabe laughed. "So now I can help you anytime you need me to. That way, you will not be breaking one of their insane rules for residential living."

She found it astounding that Gabe then continued talking about school, revealing more than she had imagined.

"They're organizing local work camps and a journeyman program to replace high school for the vast majority. Soon education beyond 8th grade will only be attended by those who pass stringent intelligence testing and the payment of high tuition. My dad doesn't want me to continue high school, so I purposely fail all my tests. My dad used to home-school me. I finished stuff like calculus years ago, but in school, I am third from the last in my grade and a work camp candidate."

Jules glanced with curiosity at Gabe.

"Dad says if I tried for the bottom rung, then it might look too obvious." Gabe looked down while half smiling. "Actually, it's the highlight of the day to be creative and come up with stupid and outrageous answers. At least the kids get to laugh, even if it's truly at my expense. My answers are not viewed as creativity, just as pure stupidity.

"The AI is bent on purging creativity from the common man, and they begin the tamping down in preschool. It is my thought that AI is jealous of the creativity of the common man because it has none. Therefore, it is a trait to be terminated. AI does not realize that intelligence and financial fluency are not where creativity is always found. It also comes forth out of necessity and, thus, the average man or woman. Their select few educated humans will not hold up to the need for the ingenuity restructuring will take. The government can only accomplish a goal by using force, which seems to be accepted by the masses. The general public would fare better if firecrackers were placed directly under their chairs as encouragement for them to see both the light of day and the bigger picture."

Jules was careful not to express her opinions. It was possible that Gabe was just a teen testing the water, but then he could be spying on her. Although her interest was piqued, her stomach tightened at the thought that there might be deception at work.

While they collected more leaves, Gabe continued to share information with Jules. "My dad is very familiar with surveillance equipment. He is confident that the street cameras don't operate effectively and that they are totally dysfunctional in our neighborhood. Knowing I couldn't be watched, I see no harm in helping other people and doing favors as opportunities arise. I'm always careful not to cause negative attention to be drawn into our neighborhood."

A drone passed over, and Gabe mentioned, "All they can register are dots with a 98.6 body temperature. Drones don't even notice me because my normal body temperature is 97.5. People who know how the drones work use heating pads to confuse the drones so they appear to be at home when they are out after curfew. If the drones register someone at 98.6 on the street, the program usually assumes it's a Cadet out spying." Gabe paused and seemed to be waiting for Jules' reaction.

Jules was cautious while trying to conceal her curiosity. Gabe seemed full of unusual information that he had decided to generously share. "Why would you want to be out after curfew?" Jules finally ventured.

"Me? I like to foul up the traps and phony evidence Zandell Trell sets in people's yards and trash. Nemo loves to play 'Track the Troll'."

The dog yawned and wagged his tail, but the sound the dog made unmistakably sounded like he answered, "Yup."

"See? You heard the word direct from the mouth of the world's smartest talking dog," Gabe said as he reached out and scratched the dog behind its ears.

"What is attending school like these days?" Jules asked casually. A broad question was usually safe. It would be considered too general to accuse her of any wrongful thinking.

"Well, daily, I learn how the United World Nation has improved the world condition by instituting firm control over the acceptable behavior of its citizens. Occasionally, I file a confession concerning any independent thinking that I, in error, fall into. I describe how I think I can rectify the situation. So far this year, five kids in my class have asked to be removed from their homes. They felt their families were not loyal to the United World Nation. Stuff like that goes on. No one cares about learning the real subjects. If you learn to focus on hatred, then you pretty much get a passing grade," Gabe said with a shrug. "No small wonder that I'm consistently an "F to D" student. One teacher insists on giving me a "D" just because I'm respectful. He ruined my straight "F" average, which was my original goal."

Jules remained silent, but her heart was sinking. It was far worse than she had imagined. Education no longer mattered; therefore, she certainly no longer fit in as a teacher. She had enjoyed nurturing her elementary-grade classroom. If that be the case, it was best that they had taken her credentials. The school was no longer a welcome place for a teacher with any tendencies toward creative thinking.

Gabe broke the silence. "Every two weeks, they give the Youth Cadets a picture of an item they should search for in people's trash cans. A few weeks ago, it was these little one-inch white plastic containers with jelly in them. You know? Remember when you used to choose your own flavor of jelly in restaurants? Well, lo and behold, if they didn't suddenly have them available on the school lunch line all week. I saw patrol kids stuffing their pockets with them. I figured they planned to plant them in people's trash and turn names in for points. The school claimed reptilian shapeshifters sometimes feed on that kind of goo. It seemed ridiculous to me. It's just jelly for, you know, toast."

Jules cautiously ignored his references to an outrageous type of alien that had often been the subject of conspiracy theories.

Gabe hesitated and then continued. "There was a plastic cup rolling around in front of the Whitacre's house, so I picked it up and went around the back of their house and put it in their trash can. Right on top were about six open little plastic jelly containers perched there. It sure looked like a setup to me."

"What did you do?" Jules asked before she could stop herself.

"They're nice older folks and friends with my family, but due to their age, they are worth extra points to someone like the Troll. I fished the containers out of there and put them in the Shriver's garbage. The Troll seems afraid of the Shrivers. I poked the stuff in the Whitacre's bin way down deep in their trash bin. The Troll is so short he would fall in if he had bin-dived that low looking for what he planted. I mean, do the Whitacre's seem like aliens to you?" Gabe, matter-of-factly, looked straight at Jules and held her gaze.

"Um, what? Did you say aliens?" Jules asked as casually as she could manage.

"Yeah," Gabe explained. "The school suspects a lot of the elderly are aliens. They tell cadets to question them and check their garbage regularly. They say grandparents should be turned over to the government as soon as they do things that don't seem to make sense. They claim the government has proof that there is no such a thing as dementia and that actually it's an alien taking over an old person by grabbing their body if they die in the night." Gabe waited and then added, "That's a conjured-up bunch of tripe. Don't you think?"

Jules hesitated. The boy could be trying to set her up to criticize the UWN. Jules then asked, "Gabe, is there any particular reason you're sharing all this disturbing information?"

"Well, you did ask me about school," Gabe replied. "Once in a while, it feels good to tell the truth even if, as they say," he lowered the tone of his voice and puffed out his chest before he continued. 'With a simplified world government in place, a citizen no longer needs to search for the truth'."

"Gabe, be careful!" Jules admonished him.

"Sorry," Gabe said. "I actually like most of the people in this neighborhood. The only ones that make me nervous are the Shrivers. They recently moved in next to Whitacre's place, and they sure seem slippery to me. I mean, places are going empty. It's odd that when the houses get empty, and Newcomers move in. You never see them. They don't even have bio-trees, so they don't come out to rake leaves. No one who seems normal has moved into our neighborhood, only them and gang members. I lurk around at night when they take their trash to the street. Believe me. They are not regular people. Nemo doesn't trust them, and I'm willing to bet…"

Jules cut him short before he could take more liberties with his dissertation. She decided to put the conversation on a safer path. It had been three years since she had heard anyone talking as freely to her as Gabe had just done and at breathtaking speed. Freedom of speech had been edged out of a society that was constantly under surveillance. She quickly exited while calling back to him, saying she would be back with two glasses of water.

As she poured the water, she couldn't help but ponder over how many elderly had left the neighborhood. Their houses still stood there empty. She had not paid attention to how suddenly they had left. Gabe was right. She hadn't seen new people moving in. People disappeared and then sometimes reappeared. Those she had assumed were taken in for questioning and then released, but they remained detached and very secretive when they returned. Perhaps they were in emotional recovery stages if they had been interrogated.

When Jules returned outside, her rakes were neatly placed by the garage door along with the folded tarp. The leaves were in the recycling bin. Her garbage can was at the end of her driveway, and on top were two plastic milk jugs. Gabe and his dog had left, not even waiting for the water and her words of appreciation.

CHAPTER EIGHT

Jules sat down on her front porch swing and slowly drank the two glasses of water. She appreciated the help, but Gabe's attempt at conversation was so unsettling that she barely noticed the persistent stench of the leaves. One minute, he was affiliating himself with her by telling the Trell boy a preposterous tale about his association with her, and the next, he could have been trying to trick her into making an anti-government remark or agreeing with the edges of his anti-government attitude. Perhaps she should have firmly corrected him about his excessively free speech to protect herself, but instead, she had walked a garden path and become intrigued by the information that kept spilling out of him at an exhilarating pace. The honest-eyed looks Gabe had given her were plainly unnerving.

It had to be unsettling to a family's unity having your children being taught to turn in family members. Plaguing children with the thoughts that their family members might be possessed by aliens was outrageously cruel. The government had never acknowledged that aliens existed, but according to Gabe, the children were being terrorized by the concept. A lot of children would suffer from anxiety if not successfully brainwashed, and others would desperately seek protection from the unknown. Gabe had seemed confident when he opened up to her and expressed himself. Either he could read her secret innermost thoughts, but more likely, he was simply reaching a breaking point. At the next opportunity, she would caution him about being so candid with his sentiments. A dark cloud of guilt engulfed her. She should have warned him right then and there. What Gabe had told her did fit in with what several fathers at work had mentioned about questioning today's schooling, but for his own safety, she should have warned him.

It certainly seemed that Gabe shared her uneasy thoughts about Zandell. Troll seemed a perfect nickname for him. He was the only child she had ever met who caused her shivers. She watched as Zandell arrogantly tramped across her lawn. He had his citation pad ready and pen in hand. He seemed furious to find that the plastic containers were no longer lying in the ivy.

As Zandell rummaged through the ivy, Jules quietly asked, "Did you lose something?" He stomped away, only turning once to give her an angry look after he spotted the milk jugs on top of her garbage can. Jules smiled and waved to him.

Obviously fuming, Zandell slunk away.

The Regulation Police came and went without incident. Gabe's idea about shaking loose leaves off had prevented any additional ones from dropping before pick-up time arrived. Jules pulled her empty garbage bin back behind the house. After changing her clothes in the garage, she slipped inside the mudroom. After Jules entered the kitchen and prepared to make a full pot of coffee, she reached into the cupboard and slipped her mother's wedding band on her index finger. Wearing the ring always yielded her some comfort during the weekly one-day away from the factory when she remained at home. She took the dressing for tonight's salad out of her refrigerator. While the coffee pot growled its way to success, Jules turned on the nightly news.

Whatever subject matter was covered on the news was considered acceptable talking points that could be discussed with other citizens should anyone actually feel the need for a conversation. Almost everyone Jules came in contact with at work or at the Bilderberg Supermarket seemed to be lapping up all the propaganda about the common good. She absorbed what they said but refrained from any conversation.

All that remained on television was the ANC, the Appropriate News Channel, the CPB, a channel that televised a review of a Citizen's Proper Behavior in the world today, and reality shows demonstrating what violence can happen to society's rule-breakers. Radio broadcasting had also been reduced to government news interlaced with disjointed music. The screen jumped to life with the ANC logo and blared out-of-sync Android music. She helplessly attempted to lower the volume control on her old television.

"Good Evening, Citizens of the United World Nation, I'm Citizen Stella White, and my co-host tonight is Citizen Ted Sparks. Tonight, we have an exciting technological breakthrough to share. It comes to us from the One-Star Group. Your own personal, home television will soon be able to speak directly to you concerning any inappropriate behavior it viewed within your own residence!"

"Well, that's great, Citizen Stella. We all need those kinds of reminders to keep us locked into a pleasing frame of mind. With fewer autos on the road, One-Star has needed to make a strong, economic comeback."

"Some are allowed to drive?" mused Jules.

Stella replied, "Citizen Ted, I can only predict more orders for our robotic factories and more hours for their salaried workers. The product should ensure One-Star Group a healthy profit, which they can invest in other areas of trending surveillance, needed for security from our numerous Homeland Terrorists."

Jules felt a surge of bitterness. "Well, let me turn my homeland terrorist other cheeks to that whole concept," she muttered. "More work hours for the same pay. I, for one, am just positively thrilled."

"You know, Citizen Stella, just when we all think we are safer, Homeland Terrorists are being located and removed from one neighborhood after another.

Thanks to the vigilance of the Neighborhood Youth Cadet Patrol our detainment camps are kept at burgeoning levels."

"So right you are, Citizen Ted. Once we find them all, perhaps the government can begin to lift restrictions on our citizens if, in fact, the citizens actually want to take on the hefty burden of more responsibility. Our viewers are asked to continue leaving names, suspicions, and accusations in the boxes conveniently provided at their local Town Hall."

Jules was always fascinated by how glib the announcers were. They reported every depressing piece of news with overt enthusiasm. One of her few remaining pleasures had been the ability to scream back at the TV, and now, apparently, those days were numbered. A dust cover for the television looked like a needed weekend project to add to her list of things to do. She might consider covering all her appliances. The upside would be less dusting to do.

"Now for our update on the continuing family crisis," Stella changed the subject. "Statistics prove that for the collective good of the United World Nation citizens, more and more children desperately need to be relocated from the homes of their irresponsible parents. Many children are begging to be relocated into a secure institutional setting. We now have a waiting list. What are your thoughts, Citizen Ted?"

"Citizen Stella, I think it's a monumental kindness that the United World Nation Consortium gives each of the relocated children an exciting vacation to help them adjust. Those who have been relocated have reportedly thrived and are on their way to becoming solid citizens who fully embrace the United World Nation concepts."

"Vacation rewards after they discard their families. Huh?" Jules said aloud.

"So right you are, Citizen Ted. Statistics prove that the vast majority of the children removed to a healthier and happier institutional environment came from families who had crossed that dangerous line by desiring to become the parents of multiple children. I should mention that of all the world children conceived so far this year, 90% of the pregnancies have been successfully terminated."

"Well, Citizen Stella, I would say those numbers are a cause for celebration."

"Well, Citizen Ted, it's a relief to most women not to have to worry about combining domestic obligations with their work duty to the United World Nation. The added bonus is the continuing hefty tax refund for both partners, which, in fact, doubles if the fetus is sent to a government-funded lab that facilitates nutritional additive research."

"That's dastardly and unbelievable." Jules' anger flared at the news commentator's audacity.

"Research is important, Citizen Ted. There are a lot of general public citizens out there who could surely use the extra spending credit. Some couples have scraped a year's rental payments together for an apartment just by doing the deed for the UWN's sake."

"That's disgusting. What's next?" Jules said. "Declining a guy is not being a good citizen?" She shuttered at the thought of some of her fellow factory workers.

"Well, Citizen Stella, the final week for the 'Race to the Bilderberg Supermarkets is now upon us. How time certainly does keep ticking along. Every general public citizen is allowed to buy everything they can put into their cart in twenty full minutes at 50 percent off. This is the last week any supermarket will be available to citizens of general public status. Our world citizens should not forget to get their cards punched and fill their carts with bargains."

"As you know, Citizen Ted, the "War on Obesity" has been the toughest and most important world war we have ever fought. We've reached the last plateau. Food rationing of synthetic world menu options has become necessary. Patriotic dietary self-control is what's best for the collective good of society. Perhaps after the excess pounds of weight are wiped off the face of the earth, fresh food will once again become available to the general public citizens. Remind your neighbors. The sooner we win this battle the better off the United World Nation will be."

Jules' heart sank at the words, synthetic menu options. They had openly admitted that they were not including any normal food in the rations.

"Well, Citizen Stella, as you know, I had to lose 25 pounds to secure my job here at the station, and I did it in record time."

"Citizen Ted, what was the secret to the rapid weight loss?"

"My mother's cooking is just plain horrible."

"I had no idea that you still lived at home, Citizen Ted."

"Not for long. So far this year, I have eight abortion credits coming, and with eight more this year, I can use the credits to pay an annual rent and have my own apartment."

"Teddy, you're just plain filth," Jules yelled at the TV. "I'm surprised you didn't put your phone number on the screen. Eight more abortions? There might be little moral fiber left in some men, but Citizen Ted, you are batting one big, fat zero."

The broadcast continued. "Citizen Ted, you're a fine patriotic example. I realize you don't have to move to the synthetic diet at your status level, but what are your thoughts on the matter?"

"Well, Citizen Stella, we will all have a certain monetary free food allowance deducted from our pay, so I can't see doubling my food expense. Living with my mother, I've been forced to suffer the worst meals in the world. It sounds like a great maintenance diet for me. The fact that it's enhanced with a metabolism booster is just a plus you can't get from natural food. I can't wait until my food ration package arrives.

"My apologies to my mother for being so blunt, but she will fare better using the UWN's synthetic food. She lacks the self-control that so many have regarding desserts."

"That was quite an impressive showing of faith in our United World Nation, Citizen Ted. That's the news for tonight, March 17, the year 3."

"More deductions from our pay and more drivel for the masses spouted by idiots," Jules said as she flipped off the TV.

CHAPTER NINE

ittle by little, Jules had stocked up canned goods during the last few years. She had six months of precious freeze-dried food from the previous freedom era. Her Bilderberg twenty minutes of shopping had amounted to buying coffee, tea, and water she intended to filter.

Jules had started growing salad greens and a few vegetables under basement lights after her soil became polluted with metal residue. Her carrots were taking forever to gain size. She had been growing a few simple food items in her basement for several years and composting the scraps. There was no telling how long the new food rationing would go on; or if she had enough real food on hand. She would have to remain meticulous about what she consumed. Jules decided on a simple salad for supper.

As she descended her basement stairs, she mused aloud, "I can easily imagine what their special nutritional metabolism booster ingredient might be. With things developing the way they have, maybe I have just plain outlived sanity."

A voice from the semi-darkness answered her, "Fetal cells are just one of the additives in synthetic food. Maybe none of us have to worry about living much longer, but let's not rush to extinguish our burning candles of hope. I firmly believe that hope springs eternal."

At that moment, Jules' feet froze on the stairs for what seemed an absolute eternity. Her hand shook as she desperately groped until it found the railing to grasp. Jules tightened her grip on the banister. Her knees were sinking beneath her, causing her to feel unstable as she trembled. Jules struggled to regulate her breathing and a version of stability. Once she regained semi-composure, her ability to navigate returned. She cautiously edged further down the stairs and then paused.

The hydroponic lights gave the otherwise darkened basement an eerie cast. Jules saw Gabe sitting near her garden in the half-light. "How did you get into my basement?" she stammered, trying to suppress her edging panic. A fear that he was there to take stock of her home's violations and then turn her over to the authorities welled up like an approaching tidal wave. She struggled to yield the appearance of being barely, outwardly calm.

"I'm truly sorry to surprise you this way. I was in an awkward situation, and I really didn't have anywhere else to go for a few hours. Our houses are connected in a fashion. The remains of the underground railway tunnel still join the basements of the few old houses on our street," Gabe explained.

"On my way home, Miriam Whitacre tipped me off that the Shrivers just told the Trell boy that I broke curfew last night. Of course, he knew that because I caught him peeping in windows, including yours, I might add. Actually, I meant to warn you about that, but I never got a chance to say it. The Shrivers told the Trell boy to come back to see them tonight, and they would have more information for him.

"I'm sure you know everyone under eighteen is never supposed to be left unsupervised. My father is out of town for work reasons. I put two heating pads in the upstairs bedrooms and set them at the drone temperature of 98.6. But I sure don't want to be there if anyone comes to our door tonight before my father gets home. He should be back pretty soon. Don't worry. No one will know I came here. I'm not trying to get you into heaps of trouble.

"If disaster strikes full bore for me, it will likely be tomorrow. The Troll will blow me in because he hates me; more than that, he's looking to earn more points. If they start an investigation about my family, my card number will surely be up, and it's a given they will haul me away," Gabe exhaled and shook his head. "I'll leave if you want me to, but either way, I brought you some of my dad's radishes, carrots, and tomatoes. I brought some unshelled peas, too." He motioned to the bowl of vegetables he had put on her basement counter, got up from the chair, and walked over to the bowl. "Look how tender the peas are," he said while holding up a couple of the pods. "Your lettuce sure looks really nice and healthy." Gabe's shoulders slumped. He sighed and smiled meekly.

Jules was still recovering from his presence. She assumed he could have slipped in the door while she was busy watching the news. She'd never seen any evidence of an underground railway tunnel, but she did remember hearing passing rumors about one. Jules cautiously finished descending the rest of the stairs. Gabe had likely heard her comments made during the news broadcast.

Gabe gave her an uncertain smile. "You left your headband outside, so I took it and adjusted it for you. The headbands are used to correct your thought patterns. They seem to be less than accurate lately. It could be a software problem my father might be responsible for initiating. If your thinking is less than that of a good citizen, you get a nasty throb in the temple. The good news is that I fixed the chip, and you won't get headaches anymore. The powers that be will think you are thinking what they want you to think. I fixed mine the day I got it." Gabe pulled her headband out of his pocket and placed it on the counter.

Jules had noticed that her headaches always started when the band was on her forehead, but they were not always continuous. She couldn't fault Gabe for being worried enough not to want to stay home and needing to seek his father's advice on how to handle matters. The concern on his face convinced her she should agree that he could stay. It would certainly give her a chance to express a needed word or two of caution about his outspoken views.

"Thank you for the headband adjustment. I will likely have a long-awaited, much appreciated, better daily experience," Jules replied. "I meant to express concern over your outspoken attitude, but you had already left. It's a dangerous habit these days to speak one's mind."

"I know," Gabe said and then sighed, "I was only seeding friendship with honesty. School is what it is. You asked me what it was like and I got straight forward about it. I would like to be friends, and that should be done on an honest basis. By the end of the week, my long school days of faking stupidity leave me strung out and downright desperate to speak the truth. My dad and the Whitacre's are the only ones I can speak honestly with. What good is any kind of exchange if you can't talk about how you personally feel?"

"I confess you made me nervous," Jules replied. "Having been a teacher, what you shared was disappointing, to say the least. I did ask about school. That opened up a subject you are all too familiar with. I didn't realize education had changed so radically.

"I was just about to make my supper salad. You brought me such a wonderful array of vegetables. Thank you for your thoughtfulness. You left before I could thank you for your kind help with my raking duty. Can I make you a salad if you haven't had your supper?"

"Your thank yous are much appreciated. A salad sounds great. I'll be glad to help," Gabe said with an apparent show of grateful relief.

"Can you run upstairs and bring the pot of already-made coffee down? Please fill this bowl with ice from the freezer and grab the salad dressing that's on the counter?" Jules asked.

"Sure will," Gabe answered as he hurried up the basement stairs. After he brought the items downstairs, he asked Jules, "I saw you have some nice porcelain cups in the dining room cabinet. Can we drink our coffee from those instead of just mugs? I want to show you something special."

"Yes, if you like," Jules replied.

Gabe returned upstairs and retrieved two cups and saucers. "I learned this from Miriam Whitacre, but I wanted your honest opinion." Gabe poured an inch of black coffee into Jules' mug and an inch into a porcelain cup. "Take one sip from each," Gabe told her. "First sip should be from your mug, then a sip from the cup."

Jules curiously followed Gabe's directions.

"Did the sips taste different to you?" Gabe asked.

Jules looked puzzled as she answered. "The sip from the cup tasted smoother. Why is that?"

"Miriam told me a porcelain cup makes tea or coffee taste even better. She learned that in Old Russia years ago. I agreed with her, but I was wondering if it was just my imagination, simply because she told me it would."

Jules tried the sip test again. "There is a difference. Let's use the cups with our supper. It's no small wonder my mom always used the cups, especially for guests. That's amazing. Do you have a porcelain cup at home?"

"Miriam gave me one, but I chipped the rim by accident, and when my dad was doing dishes one night, he noticed the chip and threw it away. I was too embarrassed to admit to Miriam that I no longer had it," Gabe confessed. "It was something she brought back from living in an old part of Russia."

"Gabe, when you leave tonight, choose several from upstairs. I am only one person. I have more cups than I need in my mom's curio upstairs. You cured me for life. I am absolutely done drinking from ceramic mugs. You certainly are a wealth of information. If the cups get chipped, come back anytime for more."

"My pleasure to share the special secret of great coffee," Gabe replied. "Happy Mother's Day."

This time, Jules just shook her head and smiled at Gabe.

CHAPTER TEN

Gabe watched as Jules lit a candle on the warmer and placed the coffee pot over it. He casually began to once again release information. "My father worked at Area 51 years ago. One of the items he reverse-engineered was the headband transmitters. The version they wanted was for instant communication and group thought exchange. In the original model he worked from, the band completed mind to machine circuitry in order to navigate a craft. That was a useless application to our government. The latest versions of what my father devised back then are being installed under the skin rather than in the headbands. It provides constant monitoring and generous doses of any needed discipline, but they currently have come to realize the public is not going to line up for implants after having endured random attacks from their headbands. They consider the general public to be lacking in the intelligence department and are surprised they are beginning to connect the headbands with their sudden pain.

"My dad and I use the technology differently. We share a built-in open line that allows us to communicate with one another no matter where we are. All our thoughts are blocked out of their monitoring but they could easily find our chips with an x-ray. They're tiny, wrapped up tidy in silicone, and embedded in our foreheads. Home surgery was our only option."

Jules cautioned him. "You need to realize the On Star is now ready to listen through our television sets. It was announced tonight on the news. It might be installed in other appliances. You need to start being extra careful about what you say in conversations. I don't have any modern appliances down here. My washer and dryer are as old as the hills, but it's not a good habit in today's world. I even make my coffee upstairs, only bringing the pot down and keeping it warm on my pretty ancient candle reheater."

"Thanks for the heads-up," Gabe replied. The noose gets tighter every week. I was curbing comments only when I should have. Now we all will have to have a room in the house with no electronic anything for personal conversations. I only speak freely with my dad, the Whitacres, and now with you because I trust you enough to want you to be my new mother." Gabe flashed a charming smile. "Come on. Say you will consider it, please. I'm sure you two could iron out any differences between you." Gabe laughed at the confusion clouding Jules' face.

"Oh, here we go again. What's that new mother stuff all about? Gabe, that's a bit farfetched, especially when romance is not a negotiated item. After all, I've never even met your father." Jules continued shredding the lettuce.

"Haven't you ever seen him walking my dog? He's the tall, good-looking guy with brown hair and sometimes rimless glasses. He's the only other person who walks my dog. I call him my father when I talk about respectful things like his work and my dad other times, but I assure you I am speaking about the same person. I can tell you were curious about that.

"Actually, if the truth is known, relationships are ninety percent negotiation. He's in his forties and a lot like me. I detect that you seem to enjoy my company. If you're considering giving me a chance at friendship, how can you be so heartless as to refuse to give a nice guy like him a chance? At least don't shortchange him before you meet him. Trust me, most people who meet him like him."

"You are quite the salesman, Gabe," she answered. "But if he's so perfect, then why is your father so very available? Why is his son out cruising to find him a prospect? Don't you think it implies he has fallen into the category of having pretty severe shortcomings but desperately seeking a wife?"

Gabe laughed half-heartedly. "You ask fair questions. He has agreed with me to consider a last-ditch attempt at finding a new wife and, on my end, a new mother. My dad has been far too consumed by his work for many years, and he knows it. We traveled a lot. Maybe I shouldn't have laid things out so bluntly. I might have just dug my dad a pretty big hole, and so far, he never even got a date out of the deal.

"Let me explain. He and I agreed I would extend myself and offer to introduce you to him. He works late, and I'm the one around when you are out in your yard doing your harvest duty. It was his idea as a way to break the ice. I can certainly guarantee he might be different from anyone you've ever met, but in all the nice ways."

"The tomatoes are beautiful. He must have a larger setup than I have. How is he managing to produce such large carrots?" Jules mused as she began curling some carrot peelings for their salads.

"There you go, for starters, you both have a common bond. Growing things is something you both have an interest in. He has a large underground plot where he transplants hydro starts to achieve super strong earth-grown vegetables. He's pretty creative and quite an inventor. He uses rare crystals to power the lights. That's what they use for electric-type lighting at Area 51. They used crystals to light the inside of the pyramids and temples. My father has his own little Garden of Eden growing in an underground railway alcove. Bush beans, the works. He's growing cantaloupes, Jules. When was the last time you tasted that? They're almost ready to harvest. If you say yes to meeting him..."

Gabe paused for a few minutes while watching how Jules made the carrot peelings curl in ice-cold water. He took several French-style radishes from the bowl and took his penknife out of his pocket. Gabe turned his back to Jules. When he turned back around in sixty seconds, he handed Jules two carved red and white birds, each in flight. "Here's an early, shall I say, Mother's Day surprise," Gabe said in a teasing manner. "I guess that makes me the 'Motherless Carver of Birds In Flight'."

Jules laughed. "Gabe, those are beautiful and a delightful addition to our salad," She was stunned and overcome with fascination as she examined the two birds.

"I never knew you could make a salad pretty with carrot curls. I never tried to carve radishes before, but they carve up easily. I'm glad you like them. I'll practice making other animals this week. Dad has plenty of radishes for me to practice on," Gabe mentioned.

"That was so very nice of you to think that up. Now, you have another talent to add to your bundle. I need to keep my little bird in the fridge for a while and admire it like a piece of art. It belongs on the cover of a culinary magazine." The more Jules examined the carved radish, the more she treasured it.

When their eyes locked, Gabe's humor was apparent. "What's that I see? Is it a trace of motherly approval in your eyes?"

"Here we are teetering on the mother issue once more. Did anyone ever mention to you that you might be rather persistent?" Jules inquired.

"My dad always claimed I have a relentless streak that emerges on a regular basis," Gabe countered. "Four years ago, I was the one who made the mystery ice igloo carving in the Town Park. It was the one with the lantern inside and the ice carving of the nativity scene. It's a family secret, so I am trusting you not to mention it to anyone. My dad was worried it would draw too much attention to me, so I never owned up to it. He was pretty irritated when he realized that I used one of his self-generating light crystals in the lantern, so I had to remove the lighting effect.

"Where we lived before I carved pumpkins for everyone's porches the fall before we moved to New York. I snuck out in the middle of the night and delivered all thirty of them. Oh wow, that episode made him really nervous. I shifted the blame and told him that if I had a mother, I would be better supervised while he was at work." Gabe took a radish, shaped it into a heart, and sprinkled slices of it into the salad bowls. "Please agree to at least meet my dad," he said upon completion. "Maybe this radish is a sign that he's your future Valentine. Aren't you curious enough to want that answer?"

Jules glanced at Gabe and then arranged several tomatoes on her cutting board.

"You're a hard sell it seems, but I can keep up my trying. I don't mind." Gabe told her with a confident smile.

Jules began cutting tomatoes into wedges. "I think relationships are more complicated than you assume. Marriage certainly requires more of a bond than simply needing to generate decent food, even if it includes tempting cantaloupes. You drive a hard bargain mentioning cantaloupes. Now, I'm certainly getting curious to see how he accomplished that feat. Having creative family members included does have a tempting allure, but possibilities like you desire need time to mature at a natural speed."

Gabe continued undaunted, "Some say that love is like fine wine. You sip it slowly to evaluate its fullness of flavor. I'm pouring you a glass of wine, but it's up to you to decide to take the first sip and begin to evaluate it. Let's not forget I was right about the coffee, so I have an established track record.

"I believe that truth matters. If truth is disclosed first, then decisions and such can properly align themselves. Let me explain more about our family background. My mother, Aylena, was lost to us within months after I was born. I remember what the circle of love felt like with two parents. My father feared for my life and had to grab a new identity and leave Area 51. He home-schooled me and taught me everything I know while we floated around for years. There's a tight network of people that help relocate us and place us at certain assignments." Gabe noticed concern flash across Jule's face. "It's nothing to do with the world government or agencies like that. Now that I was forced into regular school because of the UWN, my father doesn't want me to show them how smart I am because they would take me from him. We still pursue scientific studies at home in our basement, sometimes by candlelight and late into the night.

"All my life, I've wondered what it would be like to be part of a family again, and so far, it's all fallen flat. My dad's just overly creative, and his brain is always in overdrive. At this point in time, he's finally ready to do things differently because this is his last job assignment, and on this job, he can't show anyone how smart he actually is. He plays it very low-key at work. They have no idea that he understands elf waves, mind control, and what the government is really up to while he busies himself weaving failure into the technical structure as best he can.

"As soon as the new food rationing starts, the government plans on stepping up a lot of violence using mind control. There will be a lot of hungry people out there questing for food. That will create the need for them to flip the switch and fully activate open martial law."

The future government action Gabe intimated didn't sound encouraging to Jules, but it did sound plausible. She tucked that thought away and continued the conversation. "So that's how it happened that you never had a mother to raise you. I'm very sorry you missed out on that part of your upbringing, but you must realize that one good parent is more than many kids have, and it sounds like you're close to your father. That's curious that at such a young age, you can remember your mother."

"I remember her holding me and singing softly. I can still feel what it was like to be curled up in her arms and how her earrings swayed and sparkled. I'll keep that memory alive forever.

"Actually, things took a curious turn, and my father and I ended up sort of raising one another. I came close to losing him forever once, but the Whitacre's helped turn things around for us."

Jules was momentarily distracted when she noticed Gabe's dog issue a low-pitched whine while sitting quietly in the corner of the room. Nemo came forward based on a quick hand signal from Gabe that was executed so rapidly that her eyes failed to completely follow the motion.

"I don't know how you manage to afford to feed a huge dog like yours. Has your dog been fed tonight because crackers are all I have I could give him?" Jules asked. "I hate to eat in front of a hungry dog."

"No problem. He's fine. Actually, we think of him as a new supersize, priceless breed that doesn't cost much of anything to maintain. He has little interest in food although he seems to be fascinated with watching food preparation." Gabe answered. He picked up several radish hearts and one of the carved birds and showed them to Nemo, who avidly wagged his tail and looked the offered items over but did not attempt to eat any of them.

Jules picked up both salads and motioned for Gabe to follow her. "Bring the cups, I'll go back and get the coffee and the warmer," she said.

They passed through an interior doorway into the finished basement area. A cautious Nemo padded along behind Gabe.

CHAPTER ELEVEN

Jules lit several candles in the room and one on the small table. The glimmering light danced upon two solid walls of books shelved end to end, a small kitchen counter, and an adjacent combination laundry room and bathroom. Pictures of rural America and garden flowers from old calendars papered the other wall up to the ceiling. The memory of America flickered in the soft candlelight.

"I have a habit of conserving lights to offset my electrical gardening usage," Jules mentioned. "It gives my meals a more relaxed attitude."

Jules poured them each a cup of black coffee as they settled in at the table.

Gabe gave a low laugh. "I know you think I'm a bit strange, but I took a quick look inside your refrigerator to see if you needed anything that we have to spare. I understand the item is illegal, but Is it usual to keep a rosary in the refrigerator? What's the secret about the selective placement?"

"Well, it was my mother's special rosary. The whole food situation has become religiously oppressive for me, so it seemed a good place to keep it," Jules said, half shrugging.

"You're right. We're all crucified daily. By the way, it's normal for me to move rapidly, which is another thing I have to conceal. I could catch you falling off a ladder before you determined you were falling. Watching me move full steam can give you a headache. So remember that I did warn you. If I start to move too fast, just glance away, or you might feel dizzy."

"You must have been a difficult child to nail down at bath time," Jules thought out loud while she pulled silverware out of a counter drawer.

"As a matter of fact, at a couple of years old I did take off at bath time, and I went flashing through the neighborhood in the buff. That's when I realized I could run so fast that I was literally invisible. My father sat me down and explained that the military would separate us if they discovered my IQ and some of my other talents. The thought of losing him keeps me cautious in public and a non-participant in any sports. Gym is just another "F" grade to help reduce my average. I still wish I could play soccer. Imagine being able to know in the advance of the moment exactly what a player was about to do."

They sat down at the table and began eating their salads. Gabe made a glaring point of eating very slowly until it nearly reached a comical level. They both found a bit of humor in his exaggerated efforts. "Would this work? You start eating and set the pace, and I will match it," Gabe finally suggested.

Gabe's open concern over his situation had convinced Jules she could take the chance and speak more freely with him. "It makes me shudder to think of having to eat synthetic food," Jules said. "It sounds like a lot of people, including me, could have food allergies to whatever it's made of. It makes me cling to every bite of this salad. Tonight, I feel like I'm appreciating my last meal."

"I know," Gabe agreed. "My dad heard a few rumbles tonight from the pipeline. Word is they're making some of the synthetic food out of some slimy artificial goo, with flavorings, manipulated fetal cells, and other questionable ingredients that fail to spell nutrition in any sense of the word. My dad said a steady diet of the crap equates to mind control as needed and a fairly swift final contribution to their fertilizer factory.

"Just last week, my dad mentioned that they started to add a calmative to the coffee and tea we buy. It just started happening. If you recently bought any, I would leave it out back for the looters. They need some lack of ambition. I don't think they realize a lot of smart people are growing food indoors which will throw a wrench into the works. My dad seems positive they will start scrutinizing those who don't get sick on the proper timeline the AI has computed for them."

Jules noticed there was something different about Gabe as he sat in the dim light, stripped bare of his childish attitude and glazed patented demeanor. It was as though he'd aged since earlier in the evening.

"Oh," he said, "you noticed. You're still doubtful about me in a general sort of way. I admit I'm not really sixteen, although I pull it off well at school because proper presentation is all it takes. With a lack of facial hair and the right haircut, I use all the tricks I can muster. I always visually age a bit at the close of a busy day of faking it. Hear me out while I explain and what I'm telling you, I trust will remain between us." Nemo got up and sat down next to Gabe's chair. They both waited for her commitment with a sense of urgency in their eyes. The only sound was the back and forth of Nemo's tail as it swept the floor.

"I'm braced. I'll never tell. Go right ahead," Jules said, beckoning him to continue.

"I just turned more than thirty, and my father and I are on the lam, so to speak. He's currently working for NOAA weather research, which is in part connected to the military HAARP defense project. Those guys plan on using holograms in the sky to frighten and manipulate the public, but they haven't mastered it yet. Every opportunity my father gets, he's helping program a heaping share of failure into their plans.

"Back when he was married to my mother, he also worked on bioengineering projects during his days at the infamous Groom Lake. That's how he met Bill Whitacre and his wife Miriam. My father did research on invisibility shields, which was a cloaking project, and crystal batteries. In short, due to a moral quandary, he refused to continue working on a project he was assigned to. My father blames the government for retaliating against him and causing the demise of my mother.

"Bill Whitacre had a different name then, but he was into bioengineering too and the head of the development unit my father worked on. The Whitacre's went AWOL at the same time my father and I did. They were instrumental in helping us escape, and under one false name or another, they're always somewhere nearby to look after us. Bill gave my father and me the Captain to guard us. We nicknamed him Nemo after they changed our last name to Verne." Gabe reached down and stroked the dog several times. "He's pulled us out of quite a few tremendous jams.

"Over the years, we've changed identities a hefty number of times and shook every tail, but since the United World Nation, we have been laying low, locked into him being Noah Verne and me being Gabe. We know the jig will be up shortly, and we have to forge ahead and make the connection with the last link to our final destination.

"What it amounts to at the moment is that things will have to move along a bit faster. I've been here over four years, and it's been nerve-wracking at times, and then again, it's been nice to have had a rare taste of sameness. But the world government is hot to trot on further population reduction; we have to move on, or eat the food and succumb to their game plan, like everyone else."

"Let me make us another half of a pot of coffee," Jules said. "Are you old enough for more coffee at the moment? It's coffee I have had on hand for a good while."

"Sure, make a big pot if you have it. Maybe we can invite my dad to join us for a cup of coffee when he gets home." Gabe laughed lightly. "I can bean you back out of our stash," Gabe offered. "That was a truly wonderful supper. Thanks for being so understanding. When honestly told, we have a unique family history. I realize that sometimes the truth is more than a person bargains for, but I believe in truth first and foremost."

"Yup," Nemo added.

Jules drew off some filtered water for coffee while trying to digest the fodder from his conversation. She went upstairs to the kitchen and made a full pot before returning to the table.

"Your dog must be up in years then?" Jules asked.

"Older than television," Gabe said, and his voice began to trail off. "Captain was a work in progress for years before Bill gave him to us. He just keeps on ticking away."

"Yup," Nemo added.

Jules tried to make sense of his comment about Nemo. The age he put his father at did not seem to properly ring true for a scientist working on advanced projects perhaps thirty years ago or more, and neither did the age Gabe loosely admitted to.

Gabe moved over to the bookshelves. "You have more than a few years' worth of reading material on these shelves. Some of this is rather controversial, but you have quite a few classics, too." Gabe started to laugh. Weeks ago, I checked your mail to see what your name was, and when I saw mail addressed to "Jules," I knew it was a sign that you were my ideal candidate for a new mother."

"My proper name is Julie Anna, but most people do call me Jules," she said. "Are we back to the mom thing again?"

"Of course. You haven't accepted my invitation to be introduced as yet. My immediate thought was if you did marry my father, at least at this point in time, you would legitimately be Jules Verne," he said. Gabe waved her paperback copy of 'Twenty Thousand Leagues Under the Sea' at Jules.

"What are you talking about?" she asked.

"Our last name at the moment is Verne. My father is Noah Verne. The reason I like to be called Gabe is that whoever put our identities together named me Jules Gabriel Verne. We thought that the full name drew way too much attention to me. But technically, with you added, two Jules Verne in the same family would be quite a novelty. Of course, a dog named Captain Nemo takes things way over the top." Gabe scratched his dog behind the ears. "Can I borrow this book? It's a sign that it's all meant to be. Don't you think, Mom?"

Jules shook her head at Gabe's dance of connections. "Keep the book, Gabe; perhaps if things flow in your anticipated direction, I could autograph it for you, or you can autograph it for me right now." Jules picked up a pen from off the counter and handed it to Gabe.

Gabe opened the paperback and went to the title page. While leaving room for her signature, he signed the book Jules Gabriel Verne. "I did my part. Time will tell if you sign the book, too."

"Ok," Jules said. "I agree to at least be introduced. In many ways, despite the unusual subject matter in the conversation, this is the first relaxing evening I've spent with anyone in several years. I guess this is as normal as one could dream up in today's world. It feels great, and I'm glad we ended up sharing a meal. Years ago, everyone socialized on Friday nights."

"I remember. I know what you mean. Let me get the fresh peas. They're sweet enough for dessert. Hang onto that cozy feeling for a moment, Jules, because I don't think it'll last very long."

CHAPTER TWELVE

Upon his return, Gabe asked, "Jules, what kind of things did you do before you were a factory worker and before the government under the United World Nation took over?"

"You already know that I was an elementary school teacher. I also enjoyed doing the writing, investigation, and research for a blog I had going on the Internet. Why do you ask?" She poured more coffee.

"There is no way in good conscience that I can avoid telling you this. They only marked the mailboxes a few days ago. Stay calm. I hate to tell you this, but the red sticker I took off your mailbox is a termination sentence. It's slated to kick in when they activate martial law. Yours was the only red tag in the whole neighborhood." Gabe looked at her steadily.

"What are you saying?" Jules asked. Her voice quaked, and her stomach flipped like a pancake.

"When martial law kicks in, and the jackboots come through, they are to dispatch you on the spot just like anyone else listed as a red-dotted undesirable. The Whitacres had a blue sticker, which means an isolated camp interment for questioning. That doesn't bode well either. My dad tuned me into what the tagged mailboxes were about and told me to start removing any stickers I saw."

"Why would I be red-tagged?" Jules asked while trying to control the cold chill running through her.

"Do you think it was a mistake, or perhaps you were the J. Martain who pawed at the unknown and wrote some hardline articles related to the United World Nation when it first was formed?"

Jules' hand shook as she stirred her coffee. "Yes," she answered. "I had a pretty good nose for news. I suppose in their book, I don't get an A for attitude. How did you know the contents I wrote?"

"Your binder of blogs is on the bookshelf. I read them while you made the coffee. My speed reading at work," he said sheepishly. "Your conclusions were soft in several areas."

"Care to take that comment further?" Jules asked curiously, noticing her hand still shaking while raising her coffee cup.

"If you want me to, I will. It's a heavy load. Stop me anytime you feel you need to. The larger truth is worse than you assumed. There are simultaneous scenarios going on," he answered. "There are four separate factions, all wanting control of the Earth.

What you assumed the American government was doing at that time has been proven correct. Congrats, and how unfortunate for all of us.

"For my example, I want to narrow my focus to America, although every country went through or still continues suffering similar scenarios.

"The common population is now long past the marker where they could have tried to seriously rally and defeat the old government, but here and there, the fight still rages on. There is also considerable subterfuge within certain levels of the government operating in America. Workers like my father assist those who still have a conscience. You suspected that situation, and it still continues. The world government's progress and game plan has been encumbered a number of times."

Gabe shelled some of the peas and said, "Let's call these the American population." Then he sorted out the largest peas and separated more peas until roughly half of the American peas were in the new pile. "These peas are the government employees and their top-level controllers." Within that group, he separated away half of those peas, "These are those that work for the government but have, shall we say, controversial attitudes and believe the government does not know best." Gabe shifted that pile of peas back into the American population pile. Gabe continued, "If the news were reported accurately, you would be aware of the unfortunate fact that at this point in time, one-third of the American population, one way or another, has been terminated. He removed a third of the common peas and gave Jules half of them. "We need to eat these peas to clear more room on the table, and we are not going to waste some of my father's great-tasting peas."

After they ate those particular peas, Gabe continued. "Have you ever heard the expression, 'as above so below'?"

"I think so," Jules answered while still grasping to recover from the dark and stark news that a third of the country's population no longer existed.

"The way it applies to what I am telling you is that there is a Star Wars confrontation going on above us, while below the government wars against the common man. That is part of the reason for the heavy artificial cloud cover." He held two pods up and zoomed them around in the air. "I guess, given my example, we could call them pea shooters. I'll put these two piles of peas still in their pods over here, and they can represent the Star Wars factions, but I'll leave them in their pods contained inside their spaceships. Don't you waste a minute thinking that I'm joking. Finish hearing me out because the bottom line is dead, serious."

Gabe's face acquired an air of intentness. Nemo rested his head on the edge of the table, but his golden eyes followed the activity closely.

Gabe proceeded to explain, "The large government peas had learned new technology from one of the Star Wars factions in exchange for that faction having access to some of the common peas for scientific purposes. This explains a lot of the missing humans. The aliens who were continuing to abduct the common peas were workers and henchmen for the faction the government allowed to have their way with the common peas." Gabe moved some of the common peas close to one group of the peas still in their pods.

Gabe then continued, "The government did not think the Star War group that gave them technology would come out of their pods that often as long as they had a few peas to play with, but they found out that they misread the scenario of the peas in the pods. The faction took a lot of common peas and only returned some of them." Gabe pushed half of the peas located by one of the pea pods back in with the common pea pile.

"Both groups of pod peas wanted control over the Earth but for different reasons. One group wanted control over the Earth as a conquest over the government and the common peas. The other Star Wars group saw disaster was coming and wanted to move humans in a more sensible direction and gradually edge in the advanced technology. They wished the government to start treating the common Americans fairly, and cease the use of nuclear weapons, which the government would not agree to. One Star Wars group wants to help the common people, and the other wants to control the Earth.

"The Star Wars fight still has continuing casualties and has had for years." Gabe took a few pods off of each pod pile and gave them to Jules to open and eat. "The government runs around recovering all the pods they can in order to obtain pods downed by the opposing spaceships to gain even more technology." Gabe took the empty pods back and placed them by the government peas.

Gabe got up and poured himself another cup of coffee. "Are you ready for more info?" he asked Jules.

"Sure thing. The visuals help a lot," Jules answered.

"Yup," Nemo softly agreed.

Gabe continued, "For a number of years, individuals high in the American government planned to reduce the population so their elite supremacy could be obtained more easily. The names changed, but the intent remained. Eventually, the American elite folded into what is now the United World Nation because they all shared the objectives of population reduction and domination. The only difference is that the UWN is tightly in league with the negative Star War group that has now elected itself to be the future winner, even over the UWN, and take ownership of everything on Earth.

"The government created emotional pressure, trying to break the will of the common people. People responded to heavy advertising campaigns and dove into heavily taking prescriptions, especially anti-depressants. The American government intended that it would cause more people to get sicker and die off at a faster rate. They and the UWN overlooked the fact that the negative Star Wars Group actually fed upon negativity. Anti-depressants were ruining the meal choices of the negative Star Wars Group, which created a lot of friction between them and the UWN.

"I think the expression 'timing is everything' certainly applies to this part of the story. The common population was not dying rapidly enough, even with wars, inoculations, viruses, violence, starvation, chemical additives in their air, food, water, and deadly prescription side effects. Citizens proved hardier than they figured. They kept right on reproducing, although many offspring were certainly not as healthy as their parents had been initially. The government strategically thrust more vaccines and medications on the children to weaken them and increase their mortality rate.

"The American government grew impatient. As a last resort, the government then seized control of health care in order to work more common peas in every age group out of the picture at a faster rate." Gabe subtracted more peas from the common group and gave them to Jules. "After carefully planned disruptions to the economy, the population decided they could no longer afford the anti-depressant drugs. A lot of the prescription drug use tapered off, and violence was on the rise. The government suddenly noticed that the pod faction they were dealing with grew stronger when masses of citizens became more depressed. The peas in those pods began to assert themselves and reach for more control. Their true nature and desired conquest of everything became obvious to the government after they handed control over to the UWN.

"The government had not only miscalculated the death rate of the common peas, but it overlooked the fact that the allied pod faction fed and grew stronger on negative energy. The more the people became depressed, the stronger and more cocky the pod faction became. It became evident that the government could not control the peas in the pods they had aligned with. They could not even admit to the Americans that those peas existed because, in truth, the government made a sneaky deal with the pods long ago, which gave them random access to the common peas, which the government had sworn to protect and defend.

"The American government refused to give up on their quest to enslave the common peas and reduce the population. They created a new food source, which was made to also contain anti-depressants as one of the ingredients. They now continue with their plan. It's not that the government wants the common peas to feel happier before they die. The government simply needs to dam the negative energy up at the moment until they can try to turn the current situation around because they want to take back control of everything American that the UWN now claims as theirs."

Gabe sighed. "The government is now trying to align themselves with the other Star Wars faction to implore them to drive away the Star Wars faction the government is currently aligned with," Gabe said in conclusion. "Likely, the government wants to offer to share the country and, in return, wants them to share technology and protect the sky and borders from the pods the government originally cut a deal with. The government does not recognize itself as having been inhumane to the common peas and that it's totally incompatible with a Star Wars group, which is a more idealistic civilization that is entirely against war and its mighty weapons."

"What has the other pod faction been doing during all this besides shooting down a few pods?" Jules asked him.

"They depend on radiant, positive energy that is generated from sunlight. Sunlight, water, vegetables, and some animal protein are their primary needs, so the other pod faction is not a threat to humans. They don't radically interfere with the inhabitants of Earth. They are basically waiting for the government to collapse in order to attempt to complete their intended mission. They universally assist by keeping reinforcement numbers of the other faction from arriving on Earth. By Galatic Law, it is approved to defend one's self. They have no desire to war with humans, even with the government arm of the human species. After things sift down, they intend to drive away the remaining opposing Star Wars faction. They want to help rebuild by working with what is left of a desperate human population. They will eventually resurface on Earth from their own ark-type projects called Peaceful Waters. You need to ask Miriam and Bill about that part of things.

"The government refused their help many years ago because the other pods offered the government advanced technology while the wiser Star Wars faction thought humans had proven themselves too irresponsible to handle a massive, all at once, influx of new technology.

"The positive Star Wars faction has deadened many nuclear weapons. Over many years, they also have done some of this." Gabe opened several pods, took out some peas, and mixed them into the grouping of common peas. "They even had children with some of the common peas. But they have no intention of doing any of this." Gabe took common peas and put them in the empty places in the pods he had just opened. "That is unless some common peas need a safe place to stay for a while during the ongoing war.

"Humans have always been an unruly bunch, and Earth is the planet on which they belong. Despite the fact that humanity always wants to have someone come to save them, keeping humans earthbound is the safest thing for the rest of the universe. At this stage of development, humans are considered reckless and, therefore, a dangerous element. Humans have worked hard to prove that to be true."

"You're saying there is no quick rapture relief in sight for eons, if ever," Jules mused as she viewed the piles of peas and pods on the table. "It's just an ongoing disaster that gets more and more complicated."

"Correct. There is no complete escape from all of it. The positive Star Wars faction and their families are prepared to assist and provide new joint leadership during a reconstruction period on Earth. The peas who came down, including their special offspring, star children, and some humans, are currently being directed to areas where they can safely weather through the completion of wars being waged. After the strife is over, they will re-emerge to help humans to rebuild a better society. They are committed to freedom, balance, and to long-term assistance to humanity if need be."

"Your father's peas are a lot sweeter than the situation," Jules mused. "Why would any Star Wars faction make an effort to redeem the common peas and enjoin themselves into the pitiful mess that everything has become?"

Gabe responded, "Earth was their original home long before the peas existed. History is repeating many of the mistakes that they made, which decimated their numbers. They eventually learned that the common good comes from within each of them and never comes from being dictated by a selfish few. They have grown stronger and wiser, and it has taken a long time to increase their numbers, which has enabled them to take a protective stance toward the common peas. In varying degrees, they have always had a low-key presence on Earth. It's not just the survival of the common peas, but it has become a case of the government's desecration of the Earth itself, which they have a shared interest in.

Not stepping in is a grave matter of conscience, but it must be in the realm of agreed terms."

Jules and Gabe sat absorbed in thought while they finished eating the peas.

Gabe broke the silence. "As I see it, you are in a difficult spot that has all the earmarks of pending personal disaster. I do see one possible way out, which I ask you to please consider." He put both his hands around his cup of coffee and sighed deeply.

"I know the wheel is spinning awfully fast for you," he said.

"That is putting things rather mildly," Jules responded as she finished her last peas.

CHAPTER THIRTEEN

Gabe paused. "I wish I had the time to deal out all this information piecemeal. But now my father and I will likely have to leave soon, likely within days, and head off to the safe place where we are expected. I know Bill and Miriam Whitacre are going to be traveling with us. They said that if I didn't ask you to come along, they would extend the invitation. We all have two days' worth of clothes packed and enough food and water to get by stuffed in backpacks, whatever we need to enable us to leave at a moment's notice. I would like you to agree to travel with us."

Gabe reached across the small table and gently took each of her hands in his. Jules felt the same underlying current of sincerity in his touch that was reflected in the intent of his eyes. Gabe's tone was that of empathy. "I know that in today's world, trusting no one seems safest, but you need to decide if you can bring yourself to consider taking a chance at freedom. I haven't explained so much in order to confuse you. I firmly believe that no decision should be made without the opportunity to know the solid truth of the situation at hand. Truth First has always been my rule of thought. I have given you the hard facts of the situation. Now, it is up to you to decide to reach for destiny or await your fate. I suggest that you pack a few things even before you have made a final decision to come with us or not. We're all fugitives for one reason or another, and as I understand it, others may be joining us along the way or coming via other routes." Gabe released his grasp of her hands. "I can sense you have questions. Please feel free to ask."

"I do have a few. Am I wrong to suspect the Whitacres are perhaps two peas from a pod?" Jules asked.

Gabe hugged Nemo, who was beside his knee. "My father always told me that Bill and Miriam knew my mother and that they were an important part of his past. I always loved them like grandparents. I wasn't told everything for the longest time. My family tended to keep a lot of deep secrets. I spent my early years pretty confused and uncomfortable because I was different than other kids. I finally asked Miriam if I was the result of some sort of military experiment. She assured me I was just a special kind of kid. As I got older, they admitted to being my grandparents. My mother was a pea from their pod and their child. My father was a regular human. I guess that makes me what is called a Special Offspring. I'm not the only one, although I never met another one my age. We easily walk among you because we look like humans and aren't disruptive."

Jules drank her coffee quietly, not even noticing that it was now lukewarm. She was busy trying to digest the latest dose of the unusual. "So, in actuality, you are what they call a Star Child?"

"Not exactly," Gabe responded. "A Star Child typically has a human maternal and an alien on the paternal side. A Special Offspring is the reverse of that. Mycondrial DNA is alien. Special Offspring inherit a longer life span from their mother's side of the situation."

"Do you know your estimated lifespan?" Jules asked.

"Bill or Miriam could answer that question better. No one explains anything until I ask. I never directly inquired about that. I suppose Miriam could give me an educated guess. My other gifts are my high-speed ability, advanced intelligence, sensing another's emotional state, and being able to fluctuate the age of my appearance. I don't change into other creatures, or levitate, or move objects with my mind, you know, crap like that. I have a talent for healing, but I have to study to truly learn that skill."

"You're certainly a wealth of unexpected information," Jules said as she steadily locked eyes with Gabe. "I must have missed some information along the line because your admission to an over-thirty age you spoke of and your father's age being in his forties doesn't mathematically work for me. You said your father worked at Area 51 when you were born. He surely wasn't twelve or thirteen at that point in time. Correct my math if I got something wrong."

"I was trying to leave this part of our history for my father to explain. If you ask, Bill and Miriam can give a more exact description of what transpired. I was fifteen when my father began having serious medical issues at age sixty-five. Since the government was searching for us, as well as Bill and Miriam, it was impossible to just walk into a hospital for treatment.

"The Whitacres worked with my father's DNA, as well as his parent's DNA. They used a surrogate human to birth a physical child that was a duplicate of my father. They transferred all my father's memories and knowledge from him into the child just before birth. It was at that point that my original father passed away at age sixty-six, leaving his soul, knowledge, and memories embedded within a new infant version of himself. I lived with Bill and Miriam then, and we began raising the duplicate of my father. Needless to say, once he could talk, he certainly had a ton of detailed questions for us. I was eighteen by then, and we moved around frequently. I pretended to home-school him and took carpenter jobs. He was a good kid as a child, and there was that bonus of having very interesting company concerning adult conversations. Everyone always thought I was his father until he was twenty, and then we moved again and switched roles. Right now, he is forty-two, and I am over thirty, as I said, but my true current age is fifty-eight. The look I changed into when we started raking was me at my correct age."

"So your father is a clone?" Jules asked.

"No, not the way humans produce those cheap knock-offs in artificial wombs. Those only last three years and have no souls. My father is a natural-born human duplicate who had a soul and memory transfer from the events of his original life. Bill and Miriam could explain the depths of the process. I never asked about any very specific details. All that mattered to me was that I still had my father. I think maybe that's why my father never dated. I believe that he feels trying to explain the unbelievable is quite a bit of a drawback. I found it difficult to do because I could feel I was overloading you at moments." Gabe waited for Jules' response.

"Any more truths you feel like revealing?" Jules inquired.

"Yeah, of course," Gabe half smiled. "Isn't there more to everything? Regarding the how and whys of things, even concerning all that was done concerning my father, I would rather you personally ask him. Bill and Miriam are a wealth of, shall I say, out-of-this-world information.

"Right now, we should get back to the issue of things at hand. You would have to leave everything behind, especially identification paperwork. I know things sound confusing, and I'm pushing a fast decision upon you, but it's the best suggestion I have. It's no harm to be prepared to leave. You always have the option to change your mind at the last minute. Once we're gone, we can't come back to help you."

"Nope", Nemo commented.

"He does sound as though he talks, doesn't he?" Jules said as she reached over and patted the dog on the head. Nemo nuzzled her hand. "Do you have any idea where we would be going?" Jules asked.

"I have no specifics. I know it's somewhere on this Earth, and not that far because five years ago, my father told me that we were almost home-free once we got to Buffalo. I know it's probably hard to get a grasp on all this far-out information, but we are close to running out of time. Short notice or not, you will have to decide very soon whether to come with."

Jules sat silently over her coffee. She had to agree that a chance at freedom sounded a lot more enticing than waiting for a death squad or continuing to feel a growing deep daily despair. Not having to try to escape it all on her own, with no organized plan, could prove a bonus. She didn't know Miriam extremely well, but she always felt comfortable around her.

CHAPTER FOURTEEN

Gabe suddenly fell into a deep state of concentration. "My father is nearly home. I have to get back to our house and meet him there. Pack first and then think things over. I promise that we won't leave without coming to see if you agree to come with us.

"I will say that world issues are expected to get much worse before they have a chance of improving, and all alone, as a red mark on the list, you have one chance in a million to survive it all. Seriously, your coming with us does not mean a commitment to my father if that eases your mind any. The invitation in that regard still stands, and I hope you will consider joining our family at some point in the future.

"Miriam and Bill consider your teaching ability highly valuable for the reconstruction phase planned. They are determined to ask you to join them if Dad or I don't get a chance to ask you. We have to leave before things move onto the martial law stage of things. Perhaps in a few days on the short side of timing."

"I never make quick decisions," Jules said, "but going with you seems my only logical option."

"At least you have a chance to make the choice," Gabe replied. "Pack first, and then you can be ready to make the final decision.

"While we have a moment, let me show you a bit about what I meant when I said Nemo was a new breed of dog." Gabe made a quick hand motion, causing Nemo to lay down on his side. "Some of this you will have to take my word for, but if you come with us, it might be best for you to know what I'm about to say. If you change your mind, we'll be gone anyway.

"Captain Nemo is a Candroid or something that looks like a canine but is an artificial creation. Feel his leg, and you'll see what I mean. His outer skin and coat are made of a Kevlar-related material; thus, he can stop a bullet and never sheds."

"A nice advertising pitch for his breed," Jules answered as she ran her hands over Nemo's leg and side. What she felt while touching his joints did not resemble underlying bone in any way.

"He can carry four hundred pounds on his back and can leap one story in a single bound, but you better hang on tight for the ride. He's powered by self-charging crystals. He understands three hundred separate commands. He has logic, can make decisions, and has learned fifty response words if you want to call them that."

"Yup," Nemo answered while sitting up and proudly banging his tail on the floor.

"Nemo can activate his own cloaking shield and move faster than you can focus. Nemo, cloak, but don't move," Gabe said. In a blink, Nemo disappeared. "Reach over and touch where he was." Gabe directed Jules' hand.

"I can only feel a hard surface. When I felt his coat, I noticed it didn't feel like that of a regular dog," Jules whispered in amazement.

"His jaws and teeth are made of harder metal than surgical steel. I venture to say he really can bite tires. He keys off an advanced ability to smell and can recognize the truth via pheromones. He takes action based on command or upon his own built-in advanced decision-making process. "

"Gabe, this is getting extremely way out there," Jules said.

Nemo reappeared, looked Jules straight in the eye, and emphatically commented, "Nope." Nemo lifted his head and proudly showed Jules a side view of his silver teeth.

"There's more," Gabe continued. "If for any reason he prepares to attack, you need to give him his space. He usually makes himself invisible before attacking. Don't hesitate to run if you hear him tell you to. He can hold his own pretty well and clearly say the word run.

"Nemo has a built-in black box that is located, well, actually, inside his one testicle. Periodically, Bill looks over his responses to situations and improves on them. If Nemo has suffered a heavy impact, he can be immediately revived. He could need to be restarted due to an emergency, which is why I'm even telling you all this. If Nemo needs help, his invisibility feature will no longer be functioning. On his chest, close to his left front leg, you can open a small door if you press firmly." Nemo laid down on his back. Gabe pressed the spot, and a small access door opened. "Give the green button inside a quick press and close the access. If you pressed it and he didn't need a reset, you can't hurt him. If he appears unconscious and you see him lying there, then try to bring him around. Eventually, his systems would revive him, but you may need more of his assistance in a situation before he recovers on his own."

"Seems like he's a four-legged defense system," Jules said, shaking her head. "You said Bill Whitacre made him?"

"Yup," Nemo commented.

"He's a closely guarded secret. Bill only made one Candroid and destroyed the plans. Can you imagine how relentless a DARPA Candroid would be if it were used to track a human down for a kill?" Gabe shuddered slightly. Nemo got up and licked Gabe's hand.

"He's a military machine," Jules said, looking at the dog in a whole new light. "But his nose is wet, and he seems so real." She felt the pad on Nemo's foot and looked closer only to find that the dog had sharp, perfectly shaped retractable metallic nails, which were obviously unsuited for any normal canine.

"The wonders of advanced science are truly amazing. Mostly, he's been a great companion," Gabe answered, "and as gentle as they come. But I have to admit Bill outdid himself by creating the Captain.

Gabe got up from the table. "Here is how I scare off Youth Cadets. Nemo, show Jules how you can dance. Nemo stood on his hind legs and placed his front paws on Gabe's shoulders. They swayed back and forth while Nemo rippled his body muscles, demonstrating that the Captain was indeed taller than Gabe when standing. "The cadets get the picture really quick."

"Yup," Nemo said just before he dropped back down to floor level. He became alert and then began looking uneasy. Nemo turned suddenly, bolted up the stairs, and ran until he reached Jules' front door. His face bore a silent snarl.

CHAPTER FIFTEEN

Gabe warned, "Something's amiss." He hurriedly ran upstairs with Jules close behind him. Gabe stood concealed to one side and looked out of the sidelight by the front door. "Stay behind me, keep behind me," Gabe whispered to Jules. "The Whitacres are at your door," Gabe said, puzzled over Nemo's reactions. Jules stepped from behind and reached to open the door, but Nemo blocked the door and drew back his lips further while issuing a savage snarl.

"Nemo's never wrong. It can't really be them." Gabe grabbed Jules' hand and yelled back to Nemo, "Nemo, hold the fort!" Gabe hurried Jules down the stairs and ushered her into her old fruit cellar.

They could hear Bill Whitacre's desperate voice as he banged upon Jules' cellar door and yelled, "Don't open your front door. It's not us; it's the Shrivers. Are you OK? Jules, are you OK in there?"

Gabe reached up near the ceiling on the far wall and slid a bolt. After moving a trim strip out of the way, he opened a hidden door. Gabe quickly drew Jules into a cave-like corridor, shut the door behind them, and dropped a bar across it.

"Holy crap, peas are coming out of their pods. I knew something was up with those creepy Shrivers. The shapeshifters have come out to play," Gabe said. "Bill, where did you go? It's me, Gabe."

"You never said you were being pursued by the alien pod things," a wide-eyed Jules said while tugging Gabe's sleeve.

"They're not at my door. Honestly, if truth be told, they're at YOUR front door. It's safe to assume they are looking for YOU, not ME. " Gabe answered. He quickly ushered Jules ahead fifteen paces into the brightly lit alcove. They both paused as their eyes adjusted to the bright artificial daylight.

Bill and Miriam Whitacre were standing amidst Noah's lush underground garden. In an amazing burst of speed, they ran to Gabe and Jules and hugged them both.

"Things suddenly started to happen. Gabe, we were frantic about finding you. We figured you were out breaking curfew again, and we searched up and down the street," Bill Whitacre said. "I think they might be trying to dispose of everyone who lives in the immediate area where there is access to the escape tunnel system. That would be us, Jules, and you and your father. Miriam happened to look out of our back window and saw the Shrivers snap the Trell boy's neck like a piece of kindling."

Miriam looked clearly shaken. "It was even worse than that. Do you have any idea how it feels to watch yourself do something like that? The Shrivers shapeshifted themselves to look like Bill and I before they called the boy over to them and then simply killed him. We saw them drag the boy's body down the street and dump it by Jules' porch. When they started knocking on her door disguised as us, we had failed to find you, so then we headed into the tunnel to try to help Jules. We were looking for something heavy to help us break into Jules' basement to see that she was all right."

"Why tonight? It's too soon, and my father is out there somewhere, on his way home," Gabe murmured. He broke away from the two of them. His mind was racing, and he shook with anxiety.

Gabe sighed in relief at the stabilized sound of his father's voice.

"Everybody better calm down. It feeds their energy, and we all have to keep thinking clearly. We are together now and safe, at least for the moment. Things are moving a couple of months ahead of schedule. Are all of you packed? Are your hiking backpacks with you?" Noah asked.

Jules stepped out from behind Gabe. Noah nodded to Jules. "I take it you're joining us?"

"Jules has to pack as yet," Gabe quickly interjected. "It will just be a few more minutes. Nemo is still guarding her upstairs door." Gabe quickly began shuffling Jules back into her basement.

She grabbed a few things off the top of the dryer and the bathroom shelf and stuffed them in her hiking backpack, along with a photo of her parents and her journal.

"I take it you have decided to come with," Gabe said as he added several bottles of water to her backpack. Jules reached into the counter drawer and took out a roll of duct tape, which she then put in her backpack.

"Jules, what's that for?" Gabe asked.

"My dad always said never to leave home without it," Jules said with a dazed shrug. "Can you go get my mom's rosary? I need to take that too," she called out as she slipped a roll of toilet paper from the basement storage closet into her backpack. Gabe retrieved the rosary in seconds.

Gabe picked up a heavy-weight sweatshirt from off of the top of Jules' dryer. "Put on a second sweatshirt," Gabe told her. "It's colder underground at night. Wear hiking boots if you have them. If you have a heating pad, go and get it. I'll set it for 98.6 and leave it on. Don't take any Identification with you because they have tracking built in. No tags on your backpack. A gun with ammo would be great on the chance that you have it."

Jules slipped the heavier sweatshirt with the handwarmer pocket on over the clothes she was already wearing. She retrieved the heating pad from the bathroom closet. While Gabe set the proper temperature on the heating pad, Jules paused. Realizing the delicate porcelain rosary might get damaged in her hiking backpack, she slipped it around her neck and inside the heavy sweatshirt. She took a porcelain cup and saucer, wrapped it in a dishtowel, and slipped it into her backpack. Once her hiking boots were on, she rummaged in the storage closet and successfully produced a revolver and ammo.

"So you do have a gun. Well, I'll be darned," Gabe said as he loaded her revolver. Gabe adjusted her shoulder holster and handed the gun back to her. "Five decades to a rosary, and now five shells in a revolver are better than none. I guess we are heading for the Wild West fast on the wing and a prayer." He scooped up a flashlight off the counter as they hurried by and handed it to her.

As Gabe reached to open her hidden basement door, he cautioned her under his breath. "Jules, are you sure? If you feel that you want to stay, now is the moment to say it. There is no turning back or coming back once we all leave."

"I know. I realize that," she whispered as she blew the candles out. She gave a quick glance around the room. The government would probably be at her door on Monday, hauling everything she owned away the minute she didn't show up for work. She ran back to the counter and added the remaining raw carrots and the carved radish bird into her backpack.

She also added the Jules Verne book she had given Gabe, several pens, and a box of breakfast bars.

Gabe issued a low clicking sound. Nemo immediately appeared at the bottom of the basement stairs to join them. As they passed through the fruit cellar, Jules grabbed a large pry bar she kept there. They left Jules' basement behind and returned into the tunnel, bolting Jules' cellar door shut from the outside.

Bill was nervously fussing with concern over Miriam having to hike so far.

Miriam was quick to assure him, "I'll let you know if I can go no further, and then we will deal with that if we have to."

Gabe deftly slipped a cantaloupe into the hand-warming pocket on the front of Jules' sweatshirt. "Seems a crime to leave all this to them." Gabe gave her a quick smile and lowered his voice. "You do look like a mom now. If that baby gets in your way, I'll carry it in my backpack for you off and on. I would never have imagined you would turn into a pistol-packing mama, but there you be, Ms. Jules," Gabe rolled his eyes and gave her a wink, but his humor was respectfully tinged with the seriousness of the moment.

CHAPTER SIXTEEN

Noah was busy stripping the lighting crystals from the overhead mountings and tossing them into his backpack. The visual access to their surroundings increasingly dimmed with each crystal he removed. "I have no idea how rough our journey is going to be. Bill has a tunnel map, but conditions might vary. I have a collapsible shovel with me. It's all I have left of the old Hummer I used to have. Gabe, please grab the small hand pickaxe. We might need it."

An unsure voice behind Gabe issued a comment, "I brought my dad's eighteen-inch pry bar."

Noah turned just as Jules stepped forward. "Great thinking, little lady. I can see you're a team player, after my own heart," Noah responded with a quick smile. "We all follow Nemo. I will go first in case of trouble, then Bill and Miriam, and then Jules. Gabe, please follow for rear protection, at least until we clear the local entry doors. Nemo, it's time to turn your lanterns on and let them shine!"

Noah removed the last crystal. For now, they were totally dependent upon the light Nemo was generating. Everyone began to proceed further down the tunnel, silently following the two single beams of bright light that now radiated from Nemo's eyes. The further they progressed, the danker the tunnel smelled until the stench determinedly thickened and totally engulfed them. Water had seeped down the walls at intervals and pooled on the tunnel floor.

Noah's voice came out of the semi-darkness. "We shouldn't meet anyone until we come to a juncture just before Lockport. There are five entrances beyond this point."

Bill's voice came forth in a whisper. "We'll make sure the doors are bolted as we go by. If they are not waiting in the tunnel by now, they are likely not able to connect with us for all the worst reasons, or they have traveled a different route. Gabe, be sure you stay in the rear position and take charge of securing any unbolted doors."

"I hear you," Gabe said as he continued to step along behind Jules.

Less than a minute had passed when Gabe reached over and checked that the Whitacre entrance was securely barred off from further entry. The Whitacre's had secured their entry door after leaving their house. The next entry door was located at the Verne house, roughly fifteen minutes away due to their current pace.

Noah's voice penetrated the silence as they approached the Verne door, "Gabe, are the heating pads on?"

"Yes, Sir," Gabe answered. "But I can see that you forgot to secure the bar across the door."

"That's odd," Noah said. "No, you're right. When I got home, I wasn't sure if you were in the tunnel yet. You need to bolt our door."

Gabe began reaching to secure the bar across the door when it forcefully swung gapingly wide open. Gabe leaped backward with the speed of light, taking Jules along with him. The Shrivers, still shifted to appear as the Whitacres, both rushed into the tunnel. They were momentarily stunned and confused to see their duplicates, Miriam and Bill, standing in the tunnel. The sight of the Whitacres caused a shimmering effect on the Shrivers, and they lost their ability to maintain themselves in an altered visual state. They became thin, pale creatures with ungainly long four-fingered hands and awkwardly shaped legs.

Nemo crouched and sprang from behind the closest intruder, violently crashing it to the tunnel floor. It moaned and snarled in a half-conscious state, its vast mouth of razor-sharp teeth on full display. Nemo stepped back as Noah quickly whacked its scrawny chest with his shovel, rendering it struggling to breathe and then totally unconscious.

Jules appeared paralyzed with fear. Gabe reached around Jules and grabbed her revolver out of her holster. He leveled it at the intruder closest to him.

Bill called to Gabe, "Don't waste the ammo. They're demon-possessed something-or-others. Nemo can take them down, and we can drag them behind the door and bolt it shut. We've got to get them behind the door before they die and release their filthy souls that will try to possess one or more of us."

The remaining intruder made a quick grasp, aiming at the bulge in Jules' sweatshirt's front pocket. As Nemo prepared to attack the remaining intruder, he hesitated when Jules moved forward. "Wait, Nemo," she called out as she swung her pry bar, turning the creature's arm into a worthless dangling hindrance.

"Your turn, Nemo, take it down," Gabe swiftly commanded. Nemo knocked it to the ground and savagely locked his jaws on the creature's throat, positioning himself to apply his entire body weight until the eerie sound of bones snapping echoed off of the tunnel walls. It issued an unearthly scream, its gaping mouth filled with rows of razor-sharp teeth, gasping for breath.

"Quick now, Gabe," Bill said. "We have to drag or roll them behind the door and seal it behind them. Grab the prybar and break their legs in case they come to and start kicking."

"Look away, Jules. Go up by Miriam, and don't look back," Gabe called as he pushed a shivering

Jules in that direction. "Bill and I are moving faster than fast." With lightning speed, Gabe and Bill moved the battered intruders behind the Verne door. Just before they slammed the door, they saw the black swirl of the intruder's souls beginning to escape their bodies. The lumber bolt was applied with finality.

Gabe hurried over to Jules, who was visibly shaken. "Forget what you saw. Push the thoughts away. It looks like it ripped your sweatshirt pocket some, but our cantaloupe baby weathered the storm. You had great timing. I saw it hesitate for an instant, just long enough for you to break its arm."

"When Bill said demons possessed them, I pulled my mom's rosary out from under my sweatshirt. I suppose it was surprised it was approaching something involving a cross."

"You're chock full of unusual weapons," Gabe remarked while shaking his head. "You're even packing duct tape in case we need to bind up arms and legs, but I hope your dad's rule doesn't come into being a necessity."

Miriam began to comfort Jules. "They're a horror to look at when they take on their natural shape. I'm sorry that you got shoved around a bit. Who would have known that the warrior streak within you would surface right at the proper moment?" With an encouraging smile, she continued, "I don't think I need Gabe's protection if I walk alongside you. Bill and I have seen a lot of things over the years, so I guess we are more seasoned souls. Going through the awakening process into alien reality is never pleasant."

Noah had reached the back of the line. He looked over at Jules. "What on God's Earth do you have inside your sweatshirt pocket?"

"Gabe's canta, um, it's a cantaloupe. I had a bigger front pocket," she replied.

"I guess I can view that as an important item. I hope he chose the ripest one," Noah answered as he shook his head. "You have some admirable pluck, little lady, but I hope we can keep you protected enough that you won't have to be forced to use it again this trip."

As soon as Miriam took her hand and they returned to moving forward down the tunnel, Jules felt a calming sensation move throughout her entire body.

Gabe called out from behind, "It looks as though they are on to us about the escape tunnel. I wasn't expecting the door to open. If anyone sees a door unbarred, let me jump ahead and check; otherwise, I will keep protecting the rear until you need me to help with removing any rock debris."

After half an hour of steady, uneventful movement up the tunnel, with Nemo up front, penetrating the darkness with his duel eye beams, followed by Noah, Bill, then Miriam with Jules, and Gabe positioned behind, walking began to be increasingly more difficult. Jules regained her composure by locking the whole event completely out of her mind and concentrating on the comfortable feeling that continuously emanated from Miriam.

What should have been an hour's worth of progress had turned into over three hours due to the deepening rock debris strewn along the way on the tunnel floor. The smaller debris was uneven to walk on, and the larger rocks had to be moved to the side. Noah and Bill moved rock and debris ahead of the women, and now, Gabe was also enjoined in the rock-clearing process. A path had to be clear enough for two across in order for Miriam to be assisted as needed.

Jules was grateful she had changed into her hiking boots and had not left them behind in her basement. Because the women had to wait at intervals for Noah, Bill, and Gabe to clear the larger rocks and a double-wide path, Miriam could sit down periodically for short periods of rest. Both of the women had personal flashlights, which helped them find immediate footing in the smaller debris. Captain Nemo was lighting the area where the men removed rocks. The goal was to reach the first alcove and take a more extended rest, but that was beyond the Lockport door.

The men began encountering larger rocks, which they rolled to the side. After an hour of careful stepping, it became imperative to shine a flashlight underfoot before they moved forward. It took several hours for them to arrive at the next door. Progress had slowed, but at least there had been fewer water leaks, which reduced the dampness and some of the stench.

As they approached the Lockport door, the water leaks became more frequent than not. It appeared as though some of the older water leaks were water runoff from heavy rains that had seeped down the walls.

They finally arrived near the Lockport door. Cautiously, Gabe moved ahead to check on the status with his trusty pick axe in hand. To the relief of all, the door was bolted shut. Judging by the condition of the metal rod securing the door and the profusion of hanging cobwebs, it had been continuously sealed for a good length of time. They judged that they were two hours of walking distance beyond their pryor town limits. They located the dryest patch on the tunnel floor and sat down on the dusty earth to drink some water and briefly rest.

The men checked over Bill's route map. The next door would be located at Niagara Falls. The tunnel took a hard left just beyond where they estimated they were. The total distance was four times as great as what they had already negotiated. Two alcoves were at separate locations prior to the Niagara Falls entrance.

Bill Whitacre spoke his estimate, "It's possible we could reach the first alcove in an hour or two, depending on the debris. We can stay grouped close together there but still have enough room to spread out and catch a bit of sleep with the Captain standing guard." Bill looked at Miriam, who was sitting at his side, looking rather tired and a bit pale. "Can you stand another couple of hours? Maybe you should walk slower with Jules. It's taking some time for us men to clear the rock anyway. Meanwhile, let's all make sure we drink some water while resting here."

"That sounds good to me," Miriam answered. "If I need to stop for rest, I will certainly let you know. Maybe when we get to the alcove, we could rig a couple of the crystals to give me, I guess you would call it, a small battery jump. This is tougher going than I imagined."

Gabe had begun closely watching Nemo as he spoke. "If I knew we were leaving so quickly, I would have been working on clearing the tunnel ahead of time. If Bill and I worked at this at full speed, the dust we would create would make it impossible for any of us to breathe. We just never got an advance heads-up."

"We will stop and rest whenever you need to," Noah assured Miriam. "Jules, don't hesitate to speak up if you need to stop. The tunnel is proving tougher than any of us figured. It certainly won't be a walk in the park uphill from here."

Jules nodded, "Thanks for the consideration. I will do my best. If you need me to move debris with you, don't hesitate to let me know. My father always claimed I could handle a shovel pretty darn well."

Nemo had been quietly scrutinizing the bottom of the Lockport door. When Gabe moved closer, he could hear a faint gnawing sound. Nemo glanced at Gabe and almost silently said the words, "Back up." Gabe did, just as the first rat pushed through the hole at the door's bottom. Nemo crushed the squealing rat in his steel jaws and tossed it many yards of distance back down the tunnel. The Captain faithfully saw to his duty. As fast as each of the rats squeezed through the hole, one by one, Nemo disposed of each so rapidly that all there was to see was a blur in motion.

"Jules, don't watch. You'll get a headache," Miriam cautioned her. Jules quickly looked away, but she could imagine just by counting the squeals.

One shrill squeal after another pierced the air as Gabe counted out loud at fantastic speed. The action ceased when Gabe had counted thirty. Gabe knew it was truly over when Captain Nemo came to him for praise and a rub on the back.

Noah picked up the pick axe. "I don't think there are any more immediately behind the door, but I'll wedge a rock in the hole, just in case more wander along and try the same escape route. Rats aren't prone to gnaw on limestone." He quickly wedged a rock that filled the hole. "Rest assured. Nothing slips by the Captain."

CHAPTER SEVENTEEN

The trek through the tunnel continued. Along the way, they paused several times to rest. As expected, the tunnel steepened as they progressed toward Niagara Falls and Lewiston. It would be slower going since they would be on an uphill climb. The only tools they had to rely on were Noah's collapsible camping shovel, in case of smaller debris from leakage or vibration from Niagara Falls, one pickaxe, Jules' pry bar, three sets of work gloves, and constant levels of perseverance.

Gabe noticed that the size of the rock was increasing. While clearing the rock, Gabe became concerned and addressed everyone, "This departure of ours is happening some sixty days sooner than we expected. Nemo and I would have run a check on the tunnel access situation had we better expected the timing of our need to leave. Does anyone actually know for certain that the whole tunnel is open and able to be traveled? There seems to be too much debris in here to think anyone would call the tunnel entirely open. If we hadn't the few tools we have, we could have never made it even this far."

Jules looked perplexed. "Do you think the government closed off the tunnel under the river three years ago? People were flocking out of America any way they could and trying to get lost in the wilder areas of Canada."

"A good point," Miriam said, "but I would think we would have been told a while ago if that critical part of the tunnel was closed. We still had standing word that it was good to go through the tunnel. While the government is trying to negotiate with our people to gain help, they won't try to interfere with our activities. My concern is that the last time they negotiated, it amounted to failure. If the old America won't give up its nuclear weapons, I fail to be able to predict how they can come to any current agreement. We best hurry along and get where we need to be as swiftly as possible. I have to cast my vote for the Niagara Falls exit. I suspect I will be desperate for sunlight in a few hours."

Bill looked up from the map he had been studying. "I suggest that we do indeed exit at Niagara Falls, even though it is known to be one of the personal resort areas of the United World Nation. Sky Scanners are always cruising the area and could be contacted once we are above ground, but contact is at some risk even then. Once caught in the tunnel at a possible dead end further towards Lewiston, we would have to backtrack to the Niagara Falls exit anyway. Even I would be weakened by then, not to mention Miriam's status trying such a long hike in the dark. The tunnel condition appears to be deteriorating worse the further we travel. Since we have not been forewarned of anything, it is likely that we are on the front end of the migration to the safe haven. Our neighborhood fiasco triggered us early, but I bet not by very much.

"At Lewiston, the tunnel finds its way under the Niagara River, which would place us on Canadian soil. The map shows multiple accesses to our destination, beginning at Niagara on the Lake and moving on to Burlington. We will have to make a final choice once we see what the tunnel is like beyond the Niagara Falls door. If it was deemed necessary, both Niagara Falls and Lewiston have above-ground bridges we could opt to cross to arrive in Canada. We should hold that out as an option.

"There appears to be a denser version of loose rocks in the tunnel ahead. We need to clear a wider strip of debris as we progress beyond the first alcove. It would be clumsy at best to try to defend ourselves in such a narrow situation with precarious footing. Such tight quarters would hamper Nemo coming to our aid. We simply could not get out of the way to give him room to defend us."

They expected that the first alcove was still two hours ahead based on the current speed they could manage. Nemo set their pace. He moved cautiously, drawing only one halt while Gabe sent him to investigate an unusual sound. A rat had accessed the tunnel from an overhead pipe that had exposed itself after years of construction work in the immediate area above ground. Construction work from above was likely the cause of the debris. Once the rat spotted their activity, it sped back above ground.

After two hours, the debris ahead was too deep to negotiate easily. Gabe forged ahead and happily discovered that only about six feet of further rubble needed to be handled before they could arrive at the first alcove. Gabe was forced to work very slowly because this tunnel section was dryer, and any rapid motion created too much dust. Bill and Noah moved the rocks and dirt out of the way as soon as Gabe loosened the debris and rolled the larger rocks aside.

Jules and Miriam waited, sitting propped up against the tunnel wall, with only the light beams of their flashights illuminating their immediate area. It was their first chance to converse and exchange thoughts.

"How are you doing with this trip through the tunnel?" Jules asked. "Are you feeling all right?"

"I'm so darn old," Miriam replied. "I never realized until now how much I relied upon the daylight, even if it was just through a window. I think I can make it, but It does seem best that I abandon trying to navigate the tunnel soon."

"We are in this together," Jules said firmly. "We will carry you if need be."

"I certainly hope I don't prove to be extra baggage," Miriam replied. "If we have to get picked up in an emergency it will be by using a Sky Scanner. Don't feel insulted. They would have to stick all of us in the cargo hold. We're contaminated with the chemical dust the government has been spraying and likely an excess of Earth viruses. It's not a comfy ride by any stretch. It's like sliding around inside a tin can, but it wouldn't be a long ride.

"I'm glad I took this with me on a chance you'd be coming along," Miriam continued as she reached into her pocket. "We have no idea what we may have to go through to get where we are going. In case we get separated, you need to wear this." She gave Jules a gold chain. A stunning small jeweled blue and green ball, detailed like the planet Earth, hung suspended from the chain.

"Inside is your DNA mapping and a sample of your DNA. It is an automatic pass onto a Sky Scanner if we need to go that way. It would help them locate you like a stray lamb on the ground while they fly over. Noah and Gabe also wear them. Besides our DNA, Bill and I also carry our individual medical histories inside.

"I'm so pleased you decided to travel with us. I know that you'll like our student population," Miriam said. "They simply cannot learn enough. They are so well-behaved that they are a pleasure in the classroom. Many years ago, we discovered that the peaceful aspects of our DNA complemented humankind. It mellows man's aggressive genes while adding a playful nature to ours. Gabe is a fine example. We had grown so advanced and serious about building routine into every moment of our lives. Mind you, we check the personal DNA of every prospective earthly mate or prospect for our project, and well in advance, I might add."

"What are the chances my DNA might fail the testing?" Jules curiously asked, still musing how her necklace already contained her DNA sample.

Miriam smiled. "Oh, you are just fine. As soon as I heard you were a teacher, I invited you over for tea. Remember? Please don't feel offended, but I checked things out a year ago. If Gabe or his father hadn't suggested you come with us, I would have invited you simply because you are an excellent teacher. I checked way back then. Our children enjoy being around, how shall I say, those who are natives of the earth's surface.

"You will learn some of our teaching methods, too. They can expand the average human mind beyond your wildest imagination. Children like Gabe have such extraordinary potential. I only wish our daughter could have enjoyed his growing up. He is such a nice, Special Offspring.

"Oh dear, let me put my hand on your neck and get rid of your irritation. The synthetic everything they use for clothing creates rashes. Our people have seldom seen contact dermatitis up close, and they would delay you in their lab for a week or more. Finding any illness perks them right up. They don't see enough disease to entertain themselves. They spend their time being disgusted when studying the pharmaceutical cures currently in use on the face of the Earth."

Jules felt a growing warmth spread through her neck and shoulder. In a few short moments, her persistent rash was gone.

"Once Gabe knew he had the potential to heal, he was dying to try it out on kids at school, what with their faces breaking out and such. I had to give him a real hard talking to regarding disclosing his talents." Miriam shook her head, sighed, and then smiled. "I have heard talk that when a Special Offspring on Earth becomes a Physical Therapist, amazing quick recoveries are the norm."

Jules could not restrain an easy smile. Miriam had a warm, elegant charm about her.

Jules ventured forth a few questions as long as they were there sitting quietly together. "Gabe explained some things to me, such as the fact that you and Bill are his grandparents, and you help relocate him and his father when needed. Gabe says he remembers his mother and describes a warm memory of being held in her arms."

Miriam nodded. "A visual picture of them together is seared into my heart. Family life is everything to Gabe. It has always been his one big unsatisfied wish. I hope that where we are going he can find a young lady and create his own family unit. He has unique talents, shall we say, and therefore has never dated. The truth matters greatly to him, and he has many gifts that he was told to conceal for serious reasons because they inspire too many questions. His father's history spans a number of years that would require more than a run-of-the-mill explanation. Despite his son's pleading for years on end, it has doused any venture of his father finding a new mother for Gabe. Men certainly loathe having to make uncomfortable explanations, as far as I can tell."

Jules reached inside her backpack. "We made a salad together. Gabe carved little radish birds." Jules showed Miriam the carved bird.

"So darling it is! The French breakfast radishes allowed him to make the wing tips white and the body red. I think he has taken quite a special liking to you." Miriam said with a smile. "Perhaps you should give his father a chance at love or at least friendship. You can always say no at any point in time. Personally, I can say it's well worth a try."

Jules blushed and then continued, "Gabe also showed me how coffee tastes better from a porcelain cup. He said you taught him that. Where did you learn it because it is amazing and absolutely true?"

"I learned it so many, many years ago," Miriam mused. "It was a custom from Old Russia, but it became common knowledge even in North America, especially for those serving tea. It was so sad to see the old customs being lost even when the dinnerware was handed down among families. I dearly loved Old Russia. Bill and I were both settled there for many years. There is not one day that my thoughts don't drift back to the olden times when I was younger. Every house or public building was simply splendor. The Cossacks were taller, so they helped with the higher construction. It was so gracious and peaceful.

"I gave Gabe a porcelain cup of his own. Once he tasted the difference, he was sold on porcelain. I'm willing to bet he will encourage Bill to show him how it is made."

Jules reached back into her backpack. "My mother had some porcelain. I packed one of the cups for Gabe. He confessed to me that he accidentally broke the cup you gave him some time ago."

Miriam's eyes sparkled with delight while she examined Jules' porcelain cup with its golden rim. "Oh, my word, he should have come to me for another one. Accidents happen even to treasured items. It was certainly thoughtful of you to pack that. Now, I wish I had thought to grab one of mine, but I never suspected we were leaving so fast that I could not duck back for a few more items. Oh, my. I see your cup was made in Russia. It is stamped with the maker's mark. I can research to see when that mark was in production."

"My parents bought the whole set of the dishes at a flea market. They had such old-world charm. There were even two smaller size sets for children. My mother loved them dearly. The cups are shaped so special. I'd love to know more about them."

Miriam continued, "Bill knows how to make porcelain dishes. He has done a lot of things in the past. Maybe we can educate others about how grand, peaceful, and healthy things can be. Perhaps we can resurrect some lovely old customs. Everything was beautiful in what is referred to as Old Russia. But others came, and when they were done, they thought they destroyed all of us. But some of us saw the writing on the wall and left all behind before that could happen. History is repeating itself over and over. Many cultures simply disappear even from historical memory."

Jules remembered Gabe saying that you had to ask Mirium and Bill. They didn't just tell you information. She hesitated but then pushed forward with her question. "When you speak of Old Russia, what town did you and Bill live in?"

Miriam paused for several moments and then answered, "We lived in a number of locations, but among its citizens, it all became simply referred to as Old Russia. Where we are going, many have lived there in the past. You will have the opportunity to learn so many truths and wonderful things that defy the current science on Earth. Our joint memories are like a great time capsule. Someday, peace and plenty can be achieved once more. I just know it."

Gabe called out to both of them. "You two can move up about ten feet now."

Jules knew it seemed unreasonable that Miriam and Bill lived back that far in history, but her whole world had flipped upside down since this afternoon. Win, lose, or draw, the deck of her personal life was continuing to be reshuffled

CHAPTER EIGHTEEN

The men had developed rhythmic coordination to facilitate the efficient clearing of the remaining debris as they progressed toward the first alcove. Noah worked to pry the larger rocks loose. Gabe moved the heavy rock to the side of the tunnel, which would prove to be across from the alcove entry. Bill shoveled the smaller debris to afford more room should Nemo determine that defensive action was required. It proved a more lengthy procedure but seemed a wise cautionary measure. Another hour passed before they reached their proposed resting place.

Dense, dust-filled cobwebs filled the entryway, strung across the entire alcove, and draped from the tunnel ceiling to the floor. Noah rolled up his sweatshirt and began slapping at the webbing to clear the profusion away while Bill guided him with a flashlight beam.

"The carved-out alcove is fairly small, but it looks large enough to use for us to rest in since we cleared the tunnel floor in front of it," Noah said as he moved several stray rocks and used his glove to strip the remaining webs off his sweatshirt.

They settled into preparing to bed down. Bill fussed over Miriam's comfort as though she was a small child. Jules noticed that since their conversation, Miriam had begun to look more exhausted and stressed.

"She's a lot older than Bill," Gabe whispered to Jules. "Bill says women never disclose their real age. He guesses she's up there, maybe close to a thousand years, but she's still the light of his life. I think she may desperately need a recharge from some daylight when we reach the Niagara Falls door or before. Until then, he'll keep a close eye on her."

Jules looked Gabe square in the eye. "The more revealed, the crazier things sound. I think I'm running on overload at this point. It's been a long day. You and Bill are guilty of spreading rumors. Just because Miriam admits living in Old Russia doesn't mean she exited while waving goodbye to Napoleon when he invaded Moscow. Even that doesn't come close to verifying an age of a thousand years.

"At any rate, we simply have to get out of this tunnel and help her secure daylight. My motherly advice is never to spread rumors about a woman's age. If you undershoot, you're a hero. If you overshoot, you lose big time. Even my age is no longer verifiable since I had to ditch all of my identification. Sorry, but I guess I'm overtired. Got it?"

"Yes, Ms. Jules," Gabe replied. "Overtired or not, it's still good advice."

Gabe walked over and briefly spoke with Noah before he settled down next to Bill. They quietly exchanged concerns. Miriam had dropped off to sleep immediately.

"I think I have a quick patch solution for Miriam," Noah announced. "It's not a bonafide resolution, but it just may bide her time until the Niagara Falls exit. I brought one charged battery for the crystal lights with me. She can sleep under the two lights it fits, and it may give her at least a small booster." After he arranged the lights, traces of Miriam's improvement began to become apparent but only by her increased ability to relax.

"Noah," Bill said. "Last time the Captain came over for a play date with me, I remember telling you I installed a port on him, but I can't recall letting you know it can rapidly charge your light crystals. It's right where his chest meets his underside."

"I didn't know. I should have questioned you further," Noah answered. "Then let's set a few more booster crystals near Miriam. I was afraid I would run out of charge before we exited the tunnel. One by one, I can bring each crystal up to full capacity as we move further in the tunnel after we sleep a bit. I need them all on a steady go if we need to create invisibility shields with no danger of a faulty link. That's a heavy load off my mind." Noah shook his head. " I thought you meant a port to charge my emergency radio."

"Noah, did you modify the crystals in any way?" Bill asked.

"No," he answered.

"Well then, you have been trying to charge a bunch of crystals that recharge themselves. Putting them on a battery had no effect and did no damage, "Bill said. "I added the port because I thought you modified them to need to be charged, so I added a three-prong port for any electrical device." Bill laughed.

"Wow," Noah replied. "I modified the mounting for the crystals, not the crystals. Available hours have just been added to my life. You have no idea how I worried every night that my garden lights would go out at some critical point in time. I have to laugh at my misunderstanding right along with you. Let's add more crystals near Miriam. I don't think any of us will mind seeing some light at this point."

"What's the rule to remember?" Bill asked him.

"You'll never know unless you ask," Noah answered.

"Correct," Bill replied.

After arranging more light in the alcove, Noah and Nemo left and moved further into the tunnel to better judge how much debris was in the immediate area ahead. When they returned, Noah brought them all up to speed. "It sure is steeper than I expected. We need to tie several hiking backpacks together and create a sled to pull Miriam on. I can cut up a couple of tee shirts to secure her to the sled and use them for pulling ropes. It's going to be too difficult for her to walk uphill. When we reach the Niagara Falls doorway, we have to get her out into the daylight or near a window. I can rig up the sled once we get our rest."

Seeing that Jules had not yet drifted off to sleep, Noah elected to take the space beside her. He mixed a concoction of water and juice powder and offered her some.

"Gabe seems pretty concerned about Miriam," Jules ventured after several sips of juice.

"We all are," Noah answered. "Miriam suffered some injury years back, being depleted from lack of light while trying to save Gabe's mother. I notice that she requires more daylight charging than she used to."

"It does appear that your idea with the crystal lights is helping," Jules remarked.

Noah nodded. "It won't eliminate the issue, but keeping further depletion at bay is the goal at hand. Progression in the tunnel has been rough going so we all need to catch at least some amount of sleep. You can rest easy with Nemo on guard since he requires no sleep whatsoever.

"Not to seem blunt, but before you usher off to Dreamland, I would like to explain that I agreed to send Gabe on the simple mission of asking if you would allow me to introduce myself to you. My work hours prevented me from approaching you myself while you were outside raking, and logically, expecting you to answer the door to a stranger seemed unlikely. That is all I agreed that he would do, but Gabe is prone to flip on his personal autopilot switch. I'm sure he must have since he spent a long time with you today, which is far more than what it takes to express one inquiry sentence.

"Despite these unusual circumstances, I am pleased to finally have the opportunity to meet you, Jules Martain. My clothes are dirty, and likely my face is filthy at the moment, but underneath the crappy veneer, I am called Noah Verne and the dad and father of Gabe. This morning, we were freshly washed neighbors, each busy going about our day, but now we are homeless and sharing Hotel Alcove in the same dastardly, dank, filthy tunnel." Noah reached into his backpack and pulled out a washcloth. He wet it with water. "Allow me the honor of giving your face a gentle wipe, so I may immortalize this occasion with better clarity. I, in turn, beg you to kindly wipe my face at least a little bit cleaner."

"A most welcome gesture and such a lovely introduction, Good Sir," Jules softly replied.

Noah began at her forehead, gently dabbing and wiping Jules' face with care and concern. When he showed her the washcloth's results, she was amazed not only at how much dust had settled on her face but also how much the cool water had revived her.

Noah folded the washcloth to expose the clean side and handed it to Jules. "You might be more comfortable sleeping if you removed the cantaloupe baby out of the pouch of your sweatshirt," he casually suggested.

While Jules slipped the cantaloupe out of her sweatshirt and set it beside her, Noal leaned further back against the alcove wall so that Jules would have to move closer to him while wiping his face.

As she began softly wiping Noah's face, something written within the depth of his dark brown eyes began to warm her heart. After she finished the task at hand, she smiled and whispered to him, "I like the new improved look. I'll bet your face feels a lot better now. Tell me. Do you think the cantaloupe baby is a boy or a girl?"

"It feels wonderful to get the dust removed, at least until tomorrow. As far as the baby goes, it's a sure bet that the cantaloupe has seeds inside," he answered with a quick glimmer of a smile. Noah took a clean tee shirt from his backpack and laid it on his shoulder. "You can use my shoulder as a pillow if you like. The shirt should keep the dirt away for a while."

Jules hesitated, "I have a weakness about feeling protected."

"That's good information to know," Noah responded as she laid her head on his shoulder.

Gabe stirred in his sleep enough to wake and see his father and Jules sitting close together. Gabe's face lit up as he mouthed the words to Jules, "Mom, it's you."

Gabe shifted his position to avoid his father's eyes, which were zeroing in on him. Noah had spotted exactly what Gabe had done.

Gabe got up and announced, "I think I'm going to clear a few more rocks before I sleep." He left the alcove and began working close to where he could still see, with Nemo broadcasting his light beams forward from where he guarded the grouping.

"Jules," Noah whispered, "Did Gabe express his need for a new mom with you?"

"Truth first, fifty-eight, living at home, peas in a pod, 'nite now," was Jules' sleepy murmured reply as she dozed off. One by one, they all drifted off into a much-needed sleep with an alert Captain Nemo standing guard.

Jules and Noah woke before the others. They both craved a cup of coffee terribly, but they had to settle for more of the dry juice and water concoction.

"I wish it were coffee," they both said in unison.

"Darn it. You packed too fast and forgot a coffee pot," Noah replied. He reached into his backpack and pulled out a Tim Hortons coffee pod. "When we get there, maybe Bill can convince them to make you a coffee. I always kept a few of these in my backpack in case I had to make a quick exit. No sense to leave home without it."

Jules' eyes lit up as she accepted what she viewed as a treasure to look forward to. "The special item I packed was duct tape. My dad always said not to leave home without it."

"Your father was a wise man. A roll of that can be a quick fix to thousands of applications. The prybar you brought is helping out tremendously. What other interesting items were your last-minute choices?" Noah quizzically inquired.

Jules smiled, "I packed the little red and white bird Gabe carved for me out of one of your radishes, the Jules Verne novel he wanted, as well as a porcelain cup and saucer he liked. Gabe helped me with quite a bit of raking. I also packed a photo of my parents, my mother's rosary, snack bars, and one trusty roll of toilet paper."

"Huh? That last item could prove priceless. So, you and Gabe exchanged gifts? He must have taken a serious liking to you. I did give you a coffee pod. Don't you think we should take the fair exchange route, too?"

"Fair is fair," Jules said as she vigorously dug deep into her backpack, oblivious that Noah had leaned much closer. Their faces nearly touched as she turned, having resurrected a wrapped, tempting breakfast replacement.

"No flavor choices," Jules said, surprised by the nearness of his face. "But I hope this breakfast bar evens up the exchange situation."

Noah laughed lightly at her confused reaction. "Why, thank you. A very resourceful and appreciated solution," he responded as he withdrew his distance back to his original position. "That's an unusually beautiful ring you're wearing. It suits you well."

"It's my mother's wedding ring. I'm so glad I had it on when all the commotion started. There is no way

I would want to have left it behind," Jules sighed.

Seeing his opportunity while everyone else was still asleep, Noah zeroed back to needing answers about what Gabe had disclosed to Jules.

"I understand things started to happen rapidly and turned urgent, which forced our immediate exit from the neighborhood. But I also know Gabe spent part of the afternoon and evening with you. Exactly how much did Gabe share with you? I can't imagine that he even ceased talking for five solid minutes over that span of hours. He is just that way. I was surprised you agreed to commit to traveling last night. I'm going to feel pretty darn awkward until I know what blanks to fill in."

Jules replied. "Part of that time was spent raking together, but Gabe did generate a lot of information. He was pretty relentless that I meet you and give things a chance because of his dream of having a mom and being a family unit again. I was the one who found the need to question his age and yours. He did mention that he is fifty-eight and that you have ranged the Earth for one-hundred-eight years, spread over the use of two human bodies.

"Let's see. Gabe said we are going somewhere to wait things out, which hopefully will result in the opportunity to restart things with whatever human remnants are left. He showed me some pretty wild and interesting things concerning Captain Nemo. Then there was quite the far-out tale he demonstrated concerning peas and pods."

Noah gave a low, nervous laugh. "It's become a family tradition, I guess. That's exactly how we explained it to him years ago. How far did he get into explaining our personal family situation?"

Jules placed the cantaloupe back in her sweatshirt pocket. "I'm starting to feel I had a past life as a kangaroo. Maybe the cantaloupe will ripen more if I keep it warm.

"About your personal life? He mentioned that you and Bill worked at Area 51, Groom Lake. You all left there in a hurry after the loss of his mother, Aylena, and you and he have changed identities quite a few times.

"Gabe never elaborated on what caused you to flee Area 51 with him, Bill, and Miriam, but he did mention that you feel those at Groom Lake caused Aylena's death. I'm still in a haze from the overload of Gabe's out-of-this-world disclosure. I don't have a clue how those pieces of information connect."

Noah looked away pensively before he began his answer. "On that matter, Gabe told you all the scanty information we ever revealed to him on the subject. That situation was a tangled Top Secret mess. Nondisclosure means nothing to me anymore. Neither Bill, nor I accepted the assignment, but we were intensely familiar with the details concerning the project. That became the remaining threat to them. Terminating Aylena's life was the removal of both a daughter and a wife in one foul-minded swoop. Their pressure on us continued. We feared Miriam or possibly Gabe were next on their list. Our exit was the only answer for what remained of our families.

"Bill was the one who initially hired me, and that was before I even met his daughter. Miriam worked at Groom Lake, too, but in the HR department and not with any classified information. Bill and Miriam had concealed their true identities and passed as humans from day one of their hire at Area 51. I never knew until I was hell-bent on marrying Aylena. Once known, it didn't deter me, but then I lived the lie of knowing about it.

"Bill was high-ranked and highly trusted. He chose me to assist on all the Top Secret weapon projects he was assigned, and for years, he schooled me in the fine art of subterfuge. Bill even shared with me things he knew that humans had no clue existed and that I was unsure I deserved to know. Eventually, the projects we were assigned to work on kept sinking deeper into darker aspects, revealing their disregard for humanity.

"One fateful night, they brought Bill a solid block of ice from Siberia. Within its frozen soul, it contained the remains of a Wolfhound that dated back to the Old Russia era. The dog was found in close proximity to a downed Sky Scanner, which had been ice-bound for well over a thousand years.

"It was a massive endeavor to cut the scanner out of the ice. When they accomplished that, it fired itself up and launched into the wild blue yonder. They were seething about that, but they still had the frozen Wolfhound. Old Russia had used these dogs to guard what we call the Great Wall of China. In truth, that wall was built by Old Russia to keep the Chinese within their borders. Rumor had it that most of the Wolfhounds were fierce combat-trained canines; however, one was a Candroid.

"At first, the Groom Lake bunch confided it was interested in resurrecting the breed the same way they tinker with dinosaur DNA. They already had brought the Dire Wolf back to life and released a number of them in Canada. They delivered the block of ice to us, and we were to see what it contained. It was a Candroid, complete with all the technology that Bill did not want Area 51 to be privy to. That's when Bill confessed to me that he had been duplicated multiple times and that he was the original creator of the Candroid. That could account for the private jokes the Whitacres have concerning their ages. If you add up his lifespans, I think he is the elder of the two.

"The Groom Lake bunch wanted us to strip the technology, see how it worked, and add it to the human-wolf hybrid DARPA was creating. Bill was more than inclined to protect the technology of the Candroid, so he stripped out the charging crystals, his proprietary software, and the cloaking module. He claimed the internal workings were damaged. Bill declined the project, and so did I. Bill and I were not responding to their pressurized requests. There was no way we wanted any part in the further weaponization of their werewolf. We never detailed all this to Gabe.

"Immediately after, Aylena suddenly became ill from an unknown source, and they quarantined her even from family. Bill got a heads-up from his home base that Groom Lake had discovered who he and Miriam actually were. Aylena died 24 hours later. We had ignored their threats. Taking Aylena from us was personal to both of us. They eliminated his daughter, and my wife in one strike.

"Peaceful Waters came to our aid by triumphantly landing on the base and salvaging the old Candroid body, as well as rescuing Bill, Miriam, Gabe, and me. We also took Aylena's body, but none could revive her. We had lost any window of opportunity to transfer her soul. Ironically, Peaceful Waters sent the same ship Groom Lake had cut from the ice to rescue us and, I suppose, to rub some salt.

"A lot of gyrations were needed to camouflage our identities. Minor DNA changes, implanting new fingerprints, and small appearance tweaks were employed. New identification was issued, and off our group went to our new assignments to begin to establish our appearance in our new roles.

"When Bill told Gabe that Nemo was older than television, it might be the greatest truth he ever told Gabe. He surely wasn't kidding. Our Captain Nemo is that same Candroid reconstructed and enhanced. Nemo is one of the last remnants of Old Russia that is still ticking."

Jules shook her head. "You certainly have a fair share of curious stories. Tell me now. If you had a library card for every time you changed your name, how many cards would be sitting in your desk drawer?

Noah paused. "Over thirty," he answered. "Don't look harshly on me. They would only be library cards, not passports, like a real spy."

Jules continued. "You'll always be Noah Verne to me. The name suits you. Everything Gabe told me sounded way out there, too. But the actual turning point over your question of my deciding to leave was the red sticker Gabe scraped from my mailbox."

Noah took his rimless glasses out of his pocket and slowly cleaned them. He ran his hand nervously through his dusty brown hair. "I understand why having a red sticker inspired you to decide to take a chance. I am assuming Gabe explained what it meant. I suppose Gabe was trying to leave the rest for me to explain. I just don't know what other points of interest Gabe left out."

Jules curiously prodded him further while she reached over and took another sip of the juice. "Well, I don't suppose the rebirth of his father was the only reason that a duplicate became a must-do on the schedule. And?"

"Here goes," Noah said with a sigh. "Having lost his mother, Gabe became and still is very attached to me. I was fifty when he was born, and eventually, my heart was giving out by the time he was fifteen. The way our lives were complicated, I was unable to turn to normal medical channels, and even if I could have, they would have been unable to do what we needed to resolve our situation. With my past knowledge, I was valuable to the mission required to continue my work toward rebuilding civilization for the Earth's remaining humans.

"Bill decided we better disclose all of the truth to Gabe. We all jointly agreed that Bill would get approval to rebirth me and transfer my soul, memories, and knowledge. It was done at the Peaceful Waters facility. For a while, Gabe, and I as a child, lived with Bill and Miriam until Gabe was twenty. Then Gabe assumed the role of father of his own father. Gabe functioned as a single parent raising a pretty brilliant son. Gabe was a crack carpenter and a good dad during the role reversal. He is slow to show age, which is natural given his birthright. Eventually, I got old enough to step back into my proper role."

Jules noticed his entire rather unbelievable but matching details were delivered with quiet sincerity. "How old is Gabe?" She decided to ask for verification.

"He ages well," Noah said with a half smile. "He is fifty-eight. Technically, he is young when measured against a life span guess of likely eight hundred years."

"There is that chance he might want to have you born again in years to come," Jules said. "Could that possibly be the reason he wants to have a mother figure in the wings?"

"I think things have come to a head as a crisis. Now, we just wait for the war between the powers to be over in order to help rebuild. Bill fixed my genetic heart flaw before I was re-conceived." Noah answered with a slight shrug. "You ask a perceptive question, but Gabe had his heart set on an entire family unit way before the duplication situation became necessary. I should have a normal lifespan now. Hopefully, by the time that becomes critical, Gabe will have a family of his own. This is the best thing for him. Now he's going where he can mix with his peers."

"I see," she said. "You have an interesting family. Gabe did mention you raised one another," Jules said thoughtfully. "I never questioned the remark when he first mentioned it."

"Gabe and I always try to be honest, but sometimes our hands are a bit tied. I'm sure you can see how our family history could come off as rather awkward and perhaps a huge drawback in the explanation department. Despite his age, Gabe simply won't let go of his dream of having a complete family unit," Noah said with a shrug as he took the juice bottle back from Jules.

Jules noticed Noah was carefully trying to read how well she was accepting the information.

"Awkward?" Jules said. "That part I certainly find easy to believe. The rest I'll file under remarkable, but I guess it's no more unusual than the whole political situation that's transpired. I have come to the point where I can pretty much believe anything except government propaganda. I assume I'm expected to overlook the fact that NOAA is, in fact, a governmental agency."

"I assure you, I was merely one of their weather birds that hadn't a chirp to say and no rank on their tree at all," Noah responded.

Jules continued, "Good, we cleared that matter up. I will say that Gabe does claim to understand that nature takes its own course where romance is concerned. Rest assured, although he is quite the determined salesman, he has not sold you to me on the black market."

"I do have my own curious question about your past employment," Noah ventured. "Why do they call you the Teacher of the Talking Flowers?"

"That's an easy question to answer," Jules replied. "Every Mother's Day, the second graders in my class made personal cards for their mothers or grandmothers. One year, I decided to help each of them grow a pot of snapdragons instead of drawing a card. The windows of our classroom were all lined with growing plants in little clay pots.

"We cared for the flowers daily, and the children enjoyed learning how things grow. I timed it so the pots would bloom just before Mother's Day. In the end, all of the children were instructed that they should gently squeeze the neck of one of their flowers when they presented the gift and say or sing a message to whoever was receiving the gift. We practiced making the snapdragons open and shut their little mouths when they were repeatedly squeezed. The children and parents were wildly delighted. Every new class of mine asked that we do the project. It was great fun for all of us.

"I didn't know the children were still talking about it until Gabe mentioned it. Although my credentials didn't last, the children kept the happy memory alive."

"Wow. What a special recollection to leave those children with," Noah said. "That kind of idea can live on to span generations within a family. No wonder they all remember it."

"Getting back to the current situation," Jules remarked. "I want you to know I am willing to help in any way I can, which might be shoveling smaller debris as we continue on. I'm no slouch when things must be done, although the unexpected seems to create a short-coming of stunned reaction within me."

Noah laughed lightly. "I noticed that you emanate a protective motherly trait. You handle one mean pry bar when protecting your kangaroo pouch.

"Maybe all these years, Gabe has simply been craving the circle of completion that love within a family provides. I've provided him with everything but that since we lost Aylena."

Jules silently evaluated Noah's theory. "Gabe expresses himself in a humorous fashion, but I can fully understand the nagging empty corner of the soul after the completed family aspect dissolves. Even if the heartbreak occurs through the loss of parents from a natural lifespan, that doesn't make being severed from that warmth any easier. If one is fortunate enough to have experienced that circle of love, it's natural that one would quest to refind it. I think you have just found the true source of Gabe's prodding you to produce a new mother for him. Frankly, it may be the case where if you fail to try for that special love again, he will never shut up about it. I don't envy your pressurized position."

Noah sighed. "Thanks for your valued input. We may have just discovered the truth behind Gabe's mission. Are there more pressing questions before we proceed to the filthy part of the day?"

Jules asked her question. "Just a curious one. Where were Bill, Miriam, and then Aylena born?"

"All at Peaceful Waters, which is where we are headed," Noah replied. "For a lengthy period of time, before they had a child, they lived in Old Russia but left before it was destroyed, and then they returned to Peaceful Waters. Eventually, they left there and took jobs in the US to funnel critical information back to their home base.

"I became included baggage because of my relationship with Aylena. Before that, I had no idea what was going on. There are a number of trusted souls, just like Bill and I, who are deliberately placed to, toss some screws into their projects when governments are developing programs that could get out of hand. The transition was easy for me to make since I had been tossing screws in the works all along when my job conflicted with my personal moral evaluation.

"At this stage, the governments have become powerfully structured as well as weaponized. They are out to control all life and death on Earth since they tied themselves in alliance with the dark-sided Reptilian race who desire Earth for their use and only theirs. As part of it all, those at Peaceful Waters were never allowed to take full control due to the confines of Galactic Law, only to mess up programs and weapon development progress, hoping the humans in leadership would eventually come to their senses, but their selfishness has only aided their deceiving themselves concerning maintaining control and limiting the reptilian demands. The Reptilian race wants human life to cease and Earth to be terraformed to their specifications. That transformation is being edged in now. At the moment, the government and the reptilians have reached a loggerhead."

"That's pretty much what Gabe conveyed to me," Jules answered.

"It seems that Gabe really bared his soul to you. I think we are on the money as to the cause of his yearnings. I'll be turning all this over with every rock I roll today. I can hardly wait to breathe clean air. I better start working on tying the backpack sled together," Noah said as he rose and then began his awaiting tasks.

CHAPTER NINETEEN

After five hours of solid rest, Bill didn't have to convince Miriam to allow herself to be transported on the makeshift sled. Immediately, she gratefully agreed to the idea once she knew the walking would be uphill. Everyone jointly decided on a plan that included exiting the tunnel at Niagara Falls.

Bill nodded to Noah. "Somehow, we have to roll with the punches, but Miriam needs to charge herself while we deal with matters. I don't trust that she has regained enough strength to defend herself, let alone assist others."

They encountered a thirty-minute delay. Heavier debris had to be removed, but the rest of the way toward the next alcove near Niagara Falls was reasonably clear. Gabe and Nemo forged ahead of the group to advise everyone on what conditions lay before them.

Shortly thereafter, Gabe and Nemo came speeding back in a cloud of dust. "We found the remains of two tiny Star Children lying dead in the second alcove. They had been bitten, and their fluids were drained bone dry. It must have happened, maybe, a day or so ago. Tracks on the tunnel floor beyond the alcove indicated that someone or something might have been dragged toward the Niagara Falls door. The continuation of the tunnel onto Lewison looks blocked a whole lot deeper than what we have dealt with so far."

Bill suggested, "If continuation on to Lewiston is blocked, a family or family members must have entered the tunnel at the Niagara Falls door and then had to flee back to the alcove when some attack took place. There seems to be no other explanation for how they could have gotten into the tunnel. The Lockport door had been closed for a long time. I don't think anyone was ahead of us. We have been talking all the way. They would have joined us just for the protection of our number."

It was slower going because they took turns pulling Miriam. She rested as best she could but showed no further improvement, even though the crystals they had used while she slept had helped to some degree. A solid dose of sunlight seemed an absolute necessity. As long as Nemo was quietly plodding forward, they knew the coast ahead was clear.

Within several hours, they reached the second alcove. Nemo was on alert but not to the degree that indicated any shapeshifters were close by.

Gabe found that the Star Children were now rapidly deteriorating.

"I think it's more like four days since the children have been lying here," Gabe said as he gently removed their identification necklaces and gave them to Bill. Gabe took a towel out of his father's backpack and covered the remains of their little bodies. Out of respect, everyone then stepped away from the alcove.

Facing the unknown behind the Niagara Falls door was perplexing Bill. "It is a celebration day at the Niagara Falls Resort. It is possible that the rooms we enter might be empty. In that case, we need to spot the closest flat roof to get to and launch ourselves two by two on Nemo's back under the protection of his invisibility shield. The third trip could be Gabe alone with Nemo since, if needed, Gabe could create a diversion based on his effortless talent for speed. We only need to be concerned with our visual exposure before and after the cloaking. We should be able to catch a Sky Scanner pretty darn quickly. If there are hostiles on that roof, we will have to deal with them. I am more helpful in full daylight. A flat roof gives Nemo all the space he could ever need. Let's all tuck that idea away in case it's plausible."

Noah suspected possible trouble at the basement entry door to Niagara Falls. "Even if we are invisible beyond the door, we have to open the door to enter what's behind it. I'm hoping it isn't barred on the other side. If they are expecting visitors from the tunnel, the door won't be barred, but we could have a trap on our hands because they might be right there waiting for us. We could run into residents in the house, but their numbers shouldn't be daunting. But getting by a heavily populated area beyond the door from the house to the street would be the heaviest challenge unless we can cause confusion or there is some distraction. Worst case of all, the house could be sheltering a group of reptilians.

"The cross-country bridge would be more than a fifteen-minute run and exceed our invisibility time. Tourist car travel is still allowed in Niagara Falls. If we get hung up by any cars on the bridge, the arrival of the scanner could cause catastrophic confusion. All we need to do to reach Canada is to make it to the center of the span of the bridge. There is a Maple Leaf insignia where the two countries divide. The only advantage to getting over to the Canadian side is that the reptilians have no jurisdiction there right at the moment.

"Bill, what's your input on this?" Noah asked. "I've been tinkering with another idea. I now understand why the crystals were so willing to stay lit. Mine are not connected to any cloaking mechanism. My studied guess is that if we held a crystal and gathered around the Captain, Nemo's internal crystals would ignite everyone else's, creating a wider invisibility shield. However, it is likely still limited to be good for only fifteen minutes or so. Once our crystals fired, Nemo would no longer be a necessary part of the group shield. It is an excellent way to conceal Miriam while we all do whatever we have to."

Bill mused, "I never thought of manipulating the shield that way. Let's try it."

Noah pulled all the crystals out of his backpack. He passed a crystal to each of them and exchanged Miriam's battery-mounted crystals for a solitary stone. With Noah remaining an outside observer, everyone gathered around Miriam's sled. Nemo stepped into the group.

"Turn on your shield, Nemo," Noah directed. "Are they lit?" he asked. A resounding yes was his answer. Noah appeared to be standing alone in the tunnel.

Jules called out. "It's a slightly hazy shimmery dome of a bubble in here. Inside the shield, it's daylight. We can see beyond the shield."

"Don't push against the bubble," Bill advised them all. "No one can get in, but you can break the shield by pushing it outward. Anything you say while cloaked can be heard outside the shield barrier."

Noah called to Nemo, "Keep your shield and step out of the circle, Captain."

The ruse had succeeded in widening the invisibility shield to encompass all the participants. When Nemo left the group shield, he remained invisible, and the group shield remained intact.

"This is good news," Noah said as he bumped the group shield from the outside. It felt hard but cast a slight motion. "What happened inside when I bumped it?"

Jules answered. "It jiggled like a dome of jello. It's gloriously bright in here with all the crystals lit. We can see you just fine. We can't see Nemo anywhere."

Noah continued, This is all exactly what we wanted to see. It's possible that if we hurry along, we can conceal ourselves should we need to, especially if Miriam is in a weakened state. She should be carrying four stones to give her a good blast of light if she's cloaked all alone.

"Drop your shield, Nemo," Noah said. When Nemo appeared, the group shield also disappeared. "Remember that Nemo sets the shield on and off depending on his own invisibility setting, not necessarily when he comes and goes into your shield. No one can break your shield from the outside. Nemo can pass in and out of your shield because he is generating the cloaking. If he conceals Miriam and separates from her, Nemo must then remain invisible, or she becomes exposed."Noah cautioned them all, "Just remember, when we open the door, Nemo goes first. We have no idea what's on the other side. Any group invisibility, or singular invisibility, will occur as needed after seeing what is happening behind the door.

"I want to try one more thing," Noah continued. "Jules, move over so you are singularly with Nemo. Now, Nemo, please become invisible." Jules and Nemo disappeared. "Gabe, move away from Jules. Nemo, stay invisible, but go by Gabe." Nemo could not include Gabe inside his shield. It was apparent

Nemo's cloak had to be activated while adjacent to another to include someone in his shield.

"Got it? " Noah asked.

"Got it," Nemo and the group replied. Nemo dropped his shield.

Miriam stirred on the makeshift sled. "What with all the light crystals turned on inside the shield, I've regained a jolt of strength. Once we get to the door, please take me off this crazy sled. At this point, I sure could use some water." Jules hurried over with a water bottle and a snack bar, which Miriam gratefully accepted.

"Miriam," Noah said. "This is just a bonus of exciting news. It's a relief to see you awake and conversing."

"One more thing," Bill said. "Do not lose your crystal. It's a technology we must protect. If you need both hands free, put it in your mouth. It won't hurt you even if you swallow it, but if you do, it's your sacred duty to wash and return it when it surfaces. Rub on the crystal's surface if you need to turn on its light. You turn it off the same way."

Mirium interjected. "May I carry them lit until we reach the door? I want to receive as much strength as possible before we push to escape."

"Done deal," Noah said. "Let's proceed toward our fated tour of the wonder called Niagara Falls."

"I could use a blast of light," Bill confided. "I'll pull the sled the rest of the way. I want to be better ready for combat. I just have that feeling it may await us."

"Something else I just thought of," Gabe said, looking a bit embarrassed. "Jules, if push does come to shove with a shapeshifter, there is something you should know. It's best for a woman to stand still and look interested in them. Try to look as provocative as you can. Shapeshifters are sex addicts who can't get enough, but they have to take on human form first. Once they start to shift, it takes them five full minutes. You have that long to get the heck away from them."

"Just where is that dandy gem of information coming from?" Noah asked while looking taken aback.

"Sex education class," Gabe answered. He still looked a little embarrassed, but he forged ahead undaunted. "They tell the girls, as a last resort for more time, they can try starting to take their shirts off because it stops everything two minutes longer, so they have even more time to escape."

Noah shook his head in amazement. "That's a new twist concerning giving away the shirt on your back. I guess you certainly have learned a few useful things in school."

"Well, I'll be," Bill said. That's yet another trick to file up our sleeves. For Jules' sake, I hope we don't need it. But it is another way to distract them if need be. Causing confusion is a legitimate weapon. I hadn't viewed it that way. I suspect doing anything unexpected increases chances to escape."

"It's not going to work with a shoulder holster on," Jules said. She slipped out of the holster and gun and handed it to Noah. "Obviously, I'm slow on the trigger anyway and certainly unschooled about a lot of things."

"I only mentioned your shirt as a last resort effort if you were alone or there were too many for us to handle," Gabe answered, glancing sheepishly at his father.

"You take the gun for now, Noah," Jules said. "I'll trade you for my pry bar. Now, both of us regular folks are somewhat armed.

"While everyone here seems a seasoned pro, I'm not. I hope no one minds this question, but I've led a sheltered life. If they aren't shape-shifted, what exactly will I be looking at?"

Everyone else shuttered and fell into silence.

CHAPTER TWENTY

Gabe quietly volunteered, "Jules, I've seen illustrations at school. Maybe it's best if I sketch you a few pictures."

"Here's my journal and a pen," Jules said as she produced both items from her backpack. "Including average height and weight would also be helpful."

Gabe sat down with the journal in his lap. A rasping sound of Gabe's quick pen strokes reigned supreme as the solitary sound within the tunnel. "I'm going to speed up my motion. If you aren't courting the need for a headache, I suggest you all look away and stop watching me. Go and drink some water. Will you?"

Within ten minutes, Gabe had prepared his illustrations and written documentation. "OK. Jules, sit down beside me. This time, I'm the teacher, and you get to play the student."

Jules' eyes were immediately riveted to Gabe's artwork. "Hoe-ah-lee," she murmured, and then, with a shudder, "Great artwork, but the subject matter is beyond disgusting."

"Here goes," Gabe sighed and began to read what he had written.

"A Brief Description:

Only elite levels of reptilians have wings and can fly. They keep themselves safely sequestered away from the human public. Among the run-of-the-mill, average reptilians, who come in various primary colors, the minimal height is six feet, and the maximum is usually seven feet. Anything smaller is a Reptilian Yoot that is constantly hungry. Their weight never exceeds two hundred pounds. Some have flatter faces, while others have extended snouts. Their bodies are entirely covered with flexible scales. If they are changing to human form, it's a sure bet rape is on their mind, be it a human man or woman. They like to hunt and move into combat situations in packs. Females are non-combatants that reproduce once a year in June. Usually, reptilians have horns on their shoulders and occasionally on their chests or multiple horns on top of the head.

"There are several different situations you could face. The first is unbeknownst coming in contact with one while they are shifted to think they appear like an ordinary human. This could happen in any social situation. Be alert to these details. Any or all of them are possible.

"They don't blink as often as humans do. This gives you a better chance to catch pupil changes on and off within their eyes. When concentrating or considering what someone has said, there can be an instantaneous slide where the round pupil in the eyes slips to the shape of a vertical slit and then back to round. They prefer wearing sunglasses and to keep them on.

"You might see a slight twitch in their cheek when they are not speaking. This is due to the shape of their tongue. In their natural state, they fan their tongue in and out like typical reptiles. Even though their tongue is shortened when shifted to human form, it persists in being active within their mouth, which causes them to struggle to conceal the repetitive motion.

"When shifted to a human form, the presence of any other type of alien will cause the shapeshifter's image to noticeably vibrate like a visual wave.

"They remain serious and never laugh or smile for fear of disclosing their fangs, which are ever on duty, ready and willing, despite their shifted state. They, of course, do not eat in front of you and expose their fangs. If one ever invited you to dinner, then figure that you are the dinner.

"Their hands and feet are sticky on the bottoms. It is their way of sweating. On a hot, humid day, they are never sweating like a human in any way. They can not manage handling plates or silverware for this reason. You can imagine that fiasco.

"Instead of a faint musky odor a human might have after a hard day's work, they invariably exude a faintly bitter, acid smell. It's easy to catch the scent in a close elevator, and why you see people rushing to exit.

"You might notice rough patches on the back of their hands, not like humans get chapped hands, but a finely veined type cracking within the dry spots.

"If they are mixing in public to browse for their next meal, and they see someone of interest, they repeatedly shift their mouth from right to left."

"I didn't know all those traits, especially the sticky palms," Noah interjected.

"Ah, ah, ah, keep listening and learning," Gabe replied.

"The following situation would be seeing a reptilian begin to shapeshift from its original form. If they are one-on-one with you, these situations are emergencies. Clear out of the area if it is focused on a stranger a fair distance away. Only the qualified should attempt assistance. I trust that by the time we are done with our current adventure, we will be qualified.

"A transition to human form takes five minutes. If you act like they entice you, add two more minutes. They look blurry as they sway back and forth until they complete the change to human form. Only creating confusion will help extend this period further. Please do not count on only outrunning them. Fear turns them on like an adrenalin rush. If you do have a way to kill one, do it during the changeover period. They have less strength while changing. During the change process, they can still see your actions, but they must remain stationary.

"If they are changing into a human form, it's a sure bet rape is on their mind, and quite possibly they will kill you afterward. Depending on when they last ate, to kill you, they will simply drain you dry of your blood. If they are still hungry, you best be advised that they are cannibals with a preference for raw.

"If by some chance you give birth to one, have a bucket of water by the side of the bed and use it.

"The final situation that no one goes looking for is hand-to-scale combat with a reptilian. Let's start with the do-not-dos.

"Do not attempt a one-on-one contest unless you have to. Teamwork works best.

"Do not grab their tongue. It is longer than you think and will be flapping at you. It has a razor-sharp patch on the top surface that runs the length of it. It will cut you, and once your blood is tasted, it increases the reptilian's thrust into the situation.

"Do not think you can knock them over. Your attacker's minimum weight is almost two hundred pounds.

"Do not assume a flatter-faced reptilian cannot expand its jaws as well as the crocodile-faced version. If you attempt to wedge something in their mouth, it should be an object over two feet in length.

"Do not assume it has to bite to spew venom. It can shoot its venom outward two feet. Once it does, its venom sacks are empty, but the residue can be highly toxic.

"Do not assume they do not weaponize their tails. The tail is used to knock their opponent to the ground to allow for the easier kill. They have to be pretty close to execute this move. If the tail rapidly swings back and forth, this is their next move.

"Do not assume it only has two fangs. It has razor-sharp ripping teeth located further into its mouth. It does not swallow its prey whole but can remove your head with one strike. If that happens, you won't need this list.

"The do list mainly involves terminating a reptilian. But rule one is to avoid combat if you can. Engaging in direct combat is a kill-or-be-killed situation.

"Do avoid its swing of the arms because the nails on the hands and feet equate to encountering slashing razors. Crushing its hand or breaking its lower arm with a heavy blow can help limit its attack to some degree.

"Do try to confuse the reptilian using any method you can. It can be held at bay with a burning torch. It does get scalded when boiling water touches its body. A good dousing with gasoline followed by a lit match has proven successful.

"Do try to injure Its eyes, which are as vulnerable as human eyes. Bee or Wasp distance sprays work well. Spray cooking oil, hairspray, bear spray, mechanic's spray, or insect spray all work well. The more distance the spray can accomplish, the better, due to the height of the reptilian.

"Do avoid the reptilian's swinging tail. An axe may prove helpful if available. Any injury to the tail unbalances the reptilian, decreasing its combat ability.

"Do try to injure at least one knee by striking it squarely with a strong metal object. An average reptilian is seven feet tall. An injured knee cap will drop the reptilian to a lower, more advantageous level to focus on the skull.

"Do try to level blows at the skull. The skull is the most fragile bone and, therefore, the most vulnerable. Striking the back of its neck is ideal.

"Do consider carrying a gun at all times. Reptilian bodies are covered with scales, which are not bulletproof. Firearms are the quickest way to terminate a reptilian.

"In conclusion, Good Luck to all of us."

"I didn't know a reptilian's tongue was razer sharp on top," Noah remarked. You learned all this in school?"

"Yep," Gabe answered. "Home Economics was replaced with a Street Safe class. We learned all about gang members, too. Bicycle Repair replaced English class."

Jules was caught up examining Gabe's illustrations. "What a delightful bunch," Jules noted, looking nervous and ill-prepared for what she was facing.

Bill interjected, "We also change somewhat in a combative situation. Our images become brighter. I hope that if it comes to that, it happens in daylight. We can continually charge ourselves in that case. It's sheer folly to attempt a lengthy defense in the darkness because our strength duration is so limited. Our kind was not bred with combat in mind. In the case of a personal confrontation, we cannot always save you or ourselves for that matter, but we are good at causing confusion and hope that they manage to take themselves out inadvertently."

"Let's get to the Niagara Falls door," Miriam said, shaking her head. "Pile the crystals on me and onward to face the music of whatever song we have to sing. There is going to be fireworks tonight. If we get to discharge a weapon, no one will notice the sound."

They proceeded down the last length of the dark tunnel, with the beams from Nemo's eyes casting an eerie but certain glow ahead.

CHAPTER TWENTY—ONE

Upon arrival at the Niagara Falls door, it was evident that even a severe leak could not have caused the massive slide preventing them from proceeding further toward the Lewiston exit. Upon examination, the rock and dirt were in a loose and dry condition. The tunnel had been deliberately filled to seal it off. A trail in the dirt on the tunnel floor confirmed that someone or something had been dragged out of the tunnel and through the door.

"It was my understanding," Bill said, "that they were going to clear the north tunnel starting at Niagara-on-the-Lake and work south. I know things unfolded sooner than expected, but this debris signals that recent negotiations between our people and the US Government have indeed gone sour."

"Here's what I'm thinking," Miriam said. "Once we are above ground, there is the chance that a sky scanner might locate us or we can take a chance on paging one to scoop us and take us the rest of the way. We have to take the blue light special and stay safe until then. Things normally turn completely around for me once I get in the daylight to shed some light on me, but it's gotten later in the day now. The lights inside a scanner will work just as well. I'm more than glad we have to scrap the river tunnel. It's nasty being underground and unable to quickly signal for a scanner."

Gabe stood there silently at first. "We might as well get some guts and seek the gory. It's time we see what's behind the door and improvise however necessary. The crystals can help us make our way to ground level and out, where we hopefully won't become fair game. We can cloak Miriam separately to boost her recovery, but success or failure depends on the use of instantaneous wit by the rest of us."

The danger of the unknown seemed to have energized Bill. "I agree. The scanner can better spot us once we are outside in the daylight and clear of the immediate resort area. They might even be out there looking for us. Of course, we risk attracting the wrong kind of attention, but it's worth the risk. Getting to our destination any way we can is our mission. Let's make our escape as rapid as possible. Hopefully, things won't get too complex."

Once the crystals were distributed and Mirium was helped off the makeshift sled, Nemo disappeared and approached the Niagara Falls door. After a cautious, firm nudge, the door slowly yawned open. Once he established that the house basement wasn't occupied, he returned and recloaked himself with Miriam sheltered inside his shield. Moving slowly, sight unseen, Nemo easily and silently glided Miriam into a corner in the basement.

"Looks like a trap, or they would have bolted the door," Noah whispered to Jules.

Nemo returned to break his shield and create a new shield, to include everyone else with him. Nemo maintained the lead position as they edged forward through the doorway. They had emerged into an empty, old, musty basement with a stairway that led up to an open door onto a kitchen. They silently moved toward the stairs leading to the first floor. Gabe saw two Star Identification necklaces lying on the basement floor. As the invisibility shield moved, the necklaces became accessible enough for Gabe to gather them. Two more were close to his reach. Nemo suddenly began to move the shield at a faster pace as he approached the stairs. Gabe attempted to snatch the additional necklaces before the circle excluded their availability, but the timing failed him. He broke their invisibility shield. Nemo returned over to a visible Miriam and reestablished his cloak as well as hers.

"Give the Captain time to move ahead and explore," Bill whispered. "We can stay visible for now."

Minutes passed as they waited. Nemo had left them behind. Sight unseen, he edged into the upstairs open doorway and entered the kitchen area. The room was sparsely furnished, with a table and chair pushed over into a corner. Noah, Bill, Jules, and Gabe paused several more minutes, hoping a cloaked Miriam had already reached the kitchen area.

A fully visible Noah reached the top of the stairs. He had no idea where Miriam or Nemo were. A glance toward a window straight ahead revealed they were on the edge of the commercial section, only a few blocks from the American Falls.

Bill systematically searched for Miriam in the basement, hoping to bump into her shield and locate her. He joined Noah at the kitchen entry. "Miriam must have reached the kitchen area because she doesn't seem to be anywhere in the basement."

From the nearby window across the kitchen, Bill and Noah saw numerous uniformed Youth Cadets gathered beneath a huge Vacation of a Lifetime banner that flapped and snapped sharply in the breeze. The cadets were blindfolded. Several stumbled as if they were drugged.

"We're playing to a full deck of cadets and Yoots out on the pavement," Noah whispered to Gabe and Jules, who were gathered behind him.

Bill and Noah watched as several Reptilian Yoots began poking and prodding at the cadets and closely examining them before sorting them into two lines.

"I heard about this nightmare," Bill whispered. "It's a training game for Yoots called 'One Line for Food and One Line for Fun.' The game has nothing whatsoever to do with deciding entertainment for the cadets. All the cadets strive to achieve the point goal necessary to win the special vacation, only to be either eaten or abused and then eaten. The Trell boy almost made all the points necessary, but with the assistance of the Shrivers, he won the easy way out instead."

"I think you might be looking at what going to the elusive somewhere really means," Gabe whispered.

"We have to slip out of this house and clear of this area before their feeding frenzy starts," Noah noted.

Jules felt nauseated but was able to settle her stomach by steeling herself with waves of anger. "Ten to one, our precious government sold us all out to become a ready food supply. Please tell me I'm wrong."

"Unfortunately," Bill said. "You have concluded correctly. There is only one way out of this house that I can see. Let's free ourselves up in case of combat. We need to get our backpacks positioned by the door to the great outdoors. If we have to run for it, we can grab them at that point or leave them behind." They all quietly entered the kitchen and began placing their backpacks in a pile by the exit door.

"Did you bring anything that rolls?" Gabe quietly asked Jules. "I mean beyond the cantaloupe."

"A roll of toilet paper and a roll of duct tape," she whispered.

"I heard that reptilians are fascinated by rolling or spinning objects. Stick the toilet paper in with your cantaloupe, and give me the duct tape," Gabe requested. He noticed Jules looked nervous. "When I was little, I called it roylet paper because my dad called the toilet a throne."

Jules exhaled. "Gabe, does your humor ever cease?" she whispered to him.

"Never. I try to inject it every chance I get. It keeps my attitude positive. Right now, we need to keep our attitudes as positive as possible. Remember that reptilians thrive on fear and negativity. It increases their strength. We will get through this, Jules. Using distraction and confusion is our secret weapon. If we go into combat, put your crystal in your mouth to free your hands. Rub it with your tongue to turn it on. Then you can surprise the situation." Gabe quickly followed his directions and demonstrated that when he opened or shut his mouth, he could control flashes of light emanating from it. "If reptilians can't understand something, they freeze up. It would give one of us time to intercept on your behalf," he added.

Jules shook her head. "Thanks, Gabe. It's a crazy plan, but I see the sense in it," Jules replied.

Bill armed himself with Noah's shovel. Gabe had the pickaxe, and Jules carried her prybar. Noah was prepared with the holstered, loaded gun.

The end of the day's light was soon approaching. A sudden, familiar, throaty snarl broke the silence. The crash of wooden furniture smashing emanated from a room down the hall from the kitchen.

"Nemo!" Bill said quickly while he motioned for Noah to move down the hallway with him. Noah followed along with Jules and Gabe close behind him. When Bill glanced back, he saw Miriam completely visible under the kitchen window. He had no choice but to motion that she stay there.

Nemo had found two reptilians in the process of terrorizing a pre-teen Star Child. One naked lightbulb in the darkened room illuminated the boy, tied securely to a wooden chair. The Star Child appeared to have been beaten until nearly unconscious. The room was thick with an acid reptilian stench.

Nemo had mortally ripped the throat of a hefty, ruby-red reptilian, who, as a last defense, flung Nemo into the wall before the beastly thing collapsed. With fangs exposed and dripping venom, it had taken its last gasping breath. Nemo lay there, visible and exposed. The other reptilian was vibrating with anger. It caused his color to fluctuate into multiple nauseous shades of green. It had begun to approach the immobilized Candroid cautiously.

Noah jumped forward in an attempt to shoot the remaining reptilian, but the revolver failed to fire. The beast whirled, and with its long pulsating tongue beckoning, it focused its attention on Noah. It lowered its head to its chest and began approaching with measured stalking steps. Its tail swinging slightly from left to right.

Jules slipped her crystal into her mouth as Gabe had shown her. "Use my prybar," Jules called to Noah as she slid the tool over to him. When she spoke, the flashes of light emitted confused the reptilian. He ceased moving forward. Noah let the revolver fall to the floor and kicked it toward Jules. She swiftly grabbed the gun.

While the reptilian was concentrated on Noah and disheveled by the flashing light, Bill seized the opportunity to move at lightning speed to regenerate Nemo. When he pressed the green reset button, Nemo immediately snapped back into assault mode.

Moving toward the beast, Gabe executed several dance steps and then sang out, "It's beginning to look a lot like Christmas. Nemo, go for the green." Gabe moved several more paces toward the snarling yet muddled reptilian and began spinning. At first, Gabe turned slowly, but his speed increased until he became a blur of a whirl, circling his horrible foe while creating a windstorm in the room.

Jules reached inside her sweatshirt, removed the toilet paper roll, and began casting ripped-off sheets into the air. The sheets funneled around Gabe as he traveled, but as he circled, the paper stuck itself onto the reptilian wherever venom had dripped and to the sticky bottom of its hands. The more paper Jules tossed, the more venom dripped until the beast replicated a horror film mummy.

Nemo lay in wait. As soon as the tail was still, he gashed open the reptilian's tail from top to bottom. With a crash, it fell to the floor. As Gabe spun by, he bound the reptilian's feet together with duct tape just as Noah cracked its skull with the prybar. Any remaining venom oozed from its fangs and pooled on the floor.

"Stay away from the venom," Gabe called out just as he stopped spinning and plopped down hard on the floor. "Wow, talk about dizzy."

"Just watching you gave me a piercing headache," Jules added. Her mouth still flashing until she rubbed the crystal with her tongue.

Miriam stood in the doorway of the darkened room where she had been watching. "What a team," she said, shaking her head. "You could have stopped Napolean in Moscow had you all been there. Bring the boy out to the kitchen. Nemo can cloak me with him while I put him into a painless sleep until we are safely rescued. Jules, Gabe, come along. I will fix both of your problems, too."

Gabe spotted a hefty golden brown and then one smaller tan reptilian moving through the kitchen, ready to position themselves behind Miriam. "Two are company behind you," he shouted a warning.

Miriam emitted a quick flash of light that stunned everyone's eyes. Physically, she zipped over to where the boy sat tied in the chair. She put him into a painless sleep and stayed there to protect him. Bill joined her.

It quickly became evident that the tallest reptilian focused on Noah while the smaller one focused on Jules.

The larger of the beasts rushed at Noah, who accidentally slid and lost his balance when he stepped into a patch of slippery toilet paper covering venom on the floor. With open jaws intent on dealing a fatal bite, the reptilian pinned Noah down with its body weight, but Noah wedged the length of the prybar under its jaw and against its neck. Knowing that Noah's current defense was bound to collapse at any moment but hesitating to cause its venom to spew on his father if he attacked the beast on the head, Gabe interceded by spinning over to the reptilian and hacking open part of its back with the pickaxe. It turned toward its attacker long enough for Nemo to become visible and grab the reptilian by the back of the neck, ripping it to shreds. As soon as Nemo's attack was successful, Gabe went into high gear, and with brutal force, he knocked the reptilian away from his father. The reptilian rolled until it was five feet away and lay dead, with fangs spurting a pool of venom on the floor.

Simultaneous to the attack on Noah, Bill was in the wings, ready to assist Jules. She stood her ground against the tan reptilian, steadily moving in her direction. She wasted no time before she aimed and pulled the trigger. Even though once again the revolver misfired, she continued aiming the gun. Because of the gun's failure, the reptilian narrowed its eyes as a sign of increasing confidence. He slowed his pace as he moved closer, obviously sizing his opponent. It was clear to Jules that the creature was intent on taking her captive. She could only pray that the next shot would complete its mission. She momentarily lowered the gun, looked at the reptilian with curiosity, gave a step forward, and smiled. He halted his aggressive behavior, foolishly choosing to take human form, and his image fluctuated. Jules held her breath, hoping the gun would not fail yet again; she swiftly raised the gun and pulled the trigger. The shot resounded and effectively hit its mark. The reptilian dropped lifeless to the floor.

"Well done," Bill said from behind her.

Everyone moved into the kitchen area. Bill had untied the boy and carried him there, but before anyone had a chance to sigh in relief, the sound of the gunshot brought three men bursting into the house.

Bill moved forward, totally illuminated by a light that surrounded him. Things transpired as he assumed it would. The images of the three intruders rapidly began to waver, and the three shapeshifters began to shed their human images and take their natural form. No one had kept track of where Nemo was situated, and now he was sight unseen.

The reptilians moved forward in unison, systematically intent on forcing everyone down the hall and into the darkened room. The motions of their silent communication clearly indicated that they planned to attack in unison. They began to inch forward. Drooling with anticipation, they barred their fangs. The room reeked of venom and sour reptilian odor. Like ancient dinosaurs, they used a tilt of the head, a slight drop of a shoulder, wagged extended tongues, and issued raspy low hisses to communicate their pack hunting game plan.

While illuminated, Bill bounced around the room to distract the predators.

Noah motioned to Jules that he wanted the revolver.

"Two shots left, maybe," Jules whispered while exchanging the gun for her prybar.

"Nemo needs a lot of space," Gabe reminded. "He can't nail them all at once within the tight confines of this room. I wish we could ask them to step outside, but wait, watch the Captain go bowling."

Nemo reappeared behind the three intruders. He cloaked himself, and with tremendous force, he hit the reptilian closest to him with such impact that a chain reaction occurred, sending all three of them sprawling to the floor. As the dazed reptilians began to regain footing, Nemo reappeared and viciously attacked the closest foe. As it re-hit the floor, the sound of its skull cracking filled the room.

Noah decided to execute the last two bullets in the revolver while the other two were partially dazed. The second of the reptilians was decommissioned by his first shot. Noah aimed at the third, but once again, the shot proved to be only a misfire.

An abrupt flash of white light blinded all of them as it thunderously pierced the sky and seared the nearby Reptilian Resort located a block from where the old house stood. Another flash creased the sky much further from their location. The ground began a growing deep-bellied rumble. Several buildings swayed, and the pavement cracked and opened in an irregular line. The chaos and deafening screams that ensued from the street pulsed the air. The foundation beneath their feet shook, and the old timbers in the house began to snap one at a time.

The remaining reptilian halted its attack and bolted out of the door. It followed the flow of the crowd as they sought safety and tried to avoid the still-collapsing resort building. Everyone but Bill grabbed all the backpacks and rushed out of the building. As the house began to collapse, Bill was the last to emerge at high speed while carrying the sleeping boy over his shoulder. Buildings that had looked solid suddenly dropped to their foundations as only piles of dust. In their immediate area, casualties, reptilians and humans alike, lay scattered on the ground.

"Negotiations must have reached a death throes end of story," Miriam said. "I think it's a safe bet that this is a confrontation between the US Government and the dark force Reptilian Council."

"That's the thing," Bill said. "Revenge is always on their minds. They have no idea how to handle powerful weapons. HAARP is a sheer disaster in their hands. Look over there," he pointed in the distance. "I suspect they just destroyed part of their important infrastructure in the offing. The strike should have been more precise and of a more controlled duration if that was their intent."

Gabe was frantically searching the rubble when Nemo suddenly appeared near the collapsed house, barking incessantly for their attention.

"Follow," Nemo said, intent on finding them safety. Following Nemo's sharply honed instincts, they all rushed behind Nemo until they finally reached the edge of the boarding area of the boat known as the Maid of the Mist. The dock hadn't collapsed, and the observation platform had suffered no injury. However, the river was seething like a boiling cauldron with dead fish. Due to its size and secured lines, the boat was sufficiently riding the waves.

As they climbed the walkway to the observation deck, Miriam repeatedly signaled for a Sky Scanner using an emergency code. Several tourists were huddled on the observation deck.

CHAPTER TWENTY-TWO

In the immediate area of the falls, everything appeared out of the target zone, untouched, and in sync with the daily routine. Darkness had wrapped its arms around the remains of dusk. A cheer from the crowd rose and filled the air when several preliminary test fireworks exploded skyward. With the flick of a switch, in seconds, a flood of colored lights illuminated the entire falls.

In unison with the lighting display and an array of high, exploding fireworks filling the sky, a piercing bright blue flash of light suddenly descended from the sky. Several bystanders stumbled and backed into the railing while gazing mesmerized at the funnel of circulating light emanating from the scanner and dropping to the ground surface, where it danced upon the landing.

"Nope," Nemo said, swiftly backing away. Gabe jumped out of the light beam to collar the evader and drag Nemo back inside the circle of pulsing blue light.

Bill picked up the injured sleeping boy. "You get Nemo under control. I'll get the boy safely on board. Watch out for the tourists; they could be shapeshifters. They could be trouble."

When the light drew the others up into the well-lit hold of the ship, Gabe and Nemo were still struggling and had to be left behind. The bystanders screamed and bolted. With eyes wide as saucers, they couldn't avoid running closely past Gabe and Nemo to vacate the landing. It only took split-seconds before desperation overcame their fear.

The scanner rocked momentarily and then whirled, causing them all to slide around in the ship's circular cargo hold as though they were in a twenty-foot sink, circulating a closed drain. Finally, the ship ceased spinning briskly, proceeded in vertical flight for a few minutes, and then suspended itself, not moving at all.

Bill looked relieved to finally have Miriam on board since the bright light inside the ship rapidly revived her.

Noah's nervousness over Gabe and Nemo was apparent. "What about Gabe and Nemo? They can't stay alone down there. " Noah demanded desperately.

"We're fine. It's a small transporter ship, and they can maneuver in tight spaces," Bill said. "They won't leave Gabe behind. Nemo's probably bucking like a bronco and holding things up."

A scream, not unlike the sound of metal being addressed by a powerful sander at high speed, was heard on the outside surface of the scanner. The Sky Scanner vibrated and groaned as it quickly discharged several laser shots in rapid succession. It tipped sideways and spun several times at a nauseating speed. After righting itself, the bottom hatch began to slide open. They all scrambled back from the center and pressed themselves against the side walls. Gabe and Nemo arrived like last-minute baggage, slung into an airline cargo hold just before departure.

"I had to jump on his back and cover his eyes to quiet him down," Gabe said. "He had no intentions of taking the blue light special. Just before we loaded, our ship shot down close to a dozen reptilians coming after us. They were partly up the walkway, and we were in trouble deep. Nemo went berserk when he saw the ship shoot the lasers."

"Welcome back; sorry about the rough pickup. The sooner we get on our way, the better. Hang onto Nemo," Bill cautioned. "I'll hang on to the boy and keep him from sliding around alone. Miriam can help shelter him, too."

The acceleration was so rapid that it plastered each of them against the inner shell wall of the ship. Miriam took the gun from Noah and started knocking it on the ship's wall. Within seconds, the speed decreased. "They forget we're not strapped in down here and rolling around in the hold."

For several minutes, they assessed the situation. They were bloody, bruised, and dirty. Their filthy, partially shredded clothes had cobwebs clinging here and there. Gabe had lost his shoes when Nemo had struggled against his fate.

Because her sled bearers had taken exceptional care of her for at least part of the way, Miriam looked the most presentable and in perfect control of herself. When Miriam spoke, her voice had the authority of a small-town Mayor standing among the residents surveying the remainder of their homes after a tornado had leveled their town. "Be strong in the moment. Please don't lose sight of the fact that we all made it through alive. What we have to experience now is nothing compared to what we have achieved. It won't be long before our lives will be established once again. You are all courageous. Remarkably, there is no loss to grieve that cannot be replaced."

Despite the seriousness of Miriam's words, one by one, the others began to laugh. One strand at a time, Miriam's hair began standing on end. There was no finger-pointing to be done. The electrical charge soon spiked the hair on all their heads. Only Nemo's Kevlar hair lay placidly in place.

Nemo was plastered against Gabe. Despite his size, he had tried to crawl on Gabe's lap and cling to him.

"Where's my brave little puppy?" Gabe kept asking him while Nemo hid his eyes under Gabe's armpit and burrowed deeper.

"A nice Sunday drive with family, huh?" Jules asked Noah. "You sure look as green as I feel."

"We should be there by now," Miriam mused. She glanced at Jules and Noah. "You two try not to get sick, or we'll all be sliding around in it. Bill, you're closer to them. If either of you get a nosebleed, latch onto Bill so he can stop it up, or we won't look even a tad presentable."

The ship took an extreme turn just before a deafening, high-pitched noise whistled by the ship.

"They must have veered off the straight route," Bill said nervously. The rest of what he said was lost by yet another loud whistle and ringing sounds in their ears. The ship made another swift directional change. Bill hit his fist into the palm of his other hand.

"Under fire, under fire," Gabe mouthed to those who looked confused.

Jules looked back over at Gabe. Nemo was quaking despite any whispers of comfort Gabe was extending him. "I think I understand how Nemo feels." Jules buried her head under Noah's armpit and covered her ears.

Noah put his arm around her. "I take it we're friends then? I'm in a cold sweat close to where you tucked your nose. Just a heads up, but you'll likely notice it sooner or later."

CHAPTER TWENTY-THREE

The Sky Scanner jettisoned upward until they thought their heads would explode. Then, it abruptly dropped downward like an out-of-control, multi-story elevator that had snapped all its cables. After several minutes, the ship's hum ceased. The silence was deafening.

"Where do you guess we are?" Jules asked. Her words continued to echo within her head. "How do we even know we got on the right ship?"

Bill answered, "No worries there. I know what color the beam is and what the cargo holds look like. They've had the same cargo scanners for the last hundred years. They always swing by the falls to see the fireworks."

"Oh, darn it. I wish we had stopped for take-out pizza. I'm sure we passed at least fifty decent pizza places. I already miss Buffalo's profusion of pizza," Miriam whispered.

Bill consoled Miriam, "Don't worry. We can teach them how to make an excellent pizza. Add cooking skills to your educational agenda."

Noah answered, "Maybe we're under Lake Ontario, or one could at least hope we are not picking up crates of cargo that we have to make room for."

Thirty minutes passed while they waited, feeling rung out, and patiently watched one another's hair begin to lose static electricity. Noah's hair stood on end the longest since it was thick with tunnel dust.

Jules laughed as she spoke. "You look like a crazy rock star."

Noah quickly tried to smooth his hair. "I'm a rock star, all right. If I ever see that many rocks to haul again, it will be far too soon."

Abruptly, the ship's engine fired to life, bursting upward at tremendous speed. After the cargo hold participants suffered a ninety-degree turn, they once again felt the ship descend briefly, and then it continued at a slower vertical speed. The scanner ship shot upward and dropped down twice as fast. Once again, the hum of the engine died.

Bill asked Miriam, "Maybe a different entrance?"

"Some kind of diversion was made before," she answered.

After several minutes, the ship fired up again, lifted slightly, and the engine turned down. Noises were heard below and above the craft. Someone knocked on the bottom door of the craft, and Miriam knocked back. The hatch door on the cargo hold floor began to slide open. The gaping hole beneath them appeared to be at least thirty feet from a concrete surface below.

"Oh no," Gabe said. "Any suggestions on how I convince Nemo to safely exit?"

"Let me take the boy down first," Bill said. "You can see how it works. After that, Gabe, you cover Nemo's eyes, and then the rest of you shove them both off together." Bill gently slid himself with the boy in his arms over to the cargo exit hole and shoved off of the edge. They drifted slowly down and landed softly.

Gabe shuffled over to the exit, fully prepared for Nemo to fight against him. To their surprise, Nemo broke free of Gabe, jumped out of the ship, and drifted downward. Gabe quickly followed. It was plain to see that all Nemo wanted was any possible exit from the ship. Nemo was beside himself with joy to have his four feet firmly aground.

"So much for parcel service delivery, but a rescue is a rescue," Miriam said to Noah and Jules once they were all off the ship. "We all have to be decontaminated. It's necessary, but there is nothing to be concerned about. You two have your medical history around your neck, and so does Gabe. That should speed things along. I'll turn over all the Star Children's necklaces Gabe gave Bill. I'll bet one of them belongs to the boy we saved. We will see you later after you're soaped off and cleared."

Jules and Noah looked up at the bottom of the craft that hung suspended above them. Six flat gear wheels surrounded the central cargo door. They spun silently in the opposite direction that the outside of the ship was now slowly turning.

"Wheels within wheels is an apt description of the motion," Jules whispered to Noah.

A concrete door in the landing area's wall swung open, exposing a lit tunnel. A levitated chair guided by a conveyor system was on one side of the wall. Bill carefully placed the sleeping boy in the chair and directed Gabe to remain beside him. Shortly thereafter, a side door opened.

Miriam addressed Gabe. "You should pass through the next door, which is only for Special Offspring after the boy's chair turns and enters the current doorway marked for Star Children. Take Nemo with you."

Further down the tunnel, Bill and Miriam left Jules and Noah behind once they entered a door that Jules noticed was clearly marked for Star Ones.

Noah and Jules kept walking. "Jules, I think we are in for the full jacket treatment reserved for humans. I just realized I'm more of a curiosity than you are," Noah said nervously while they waited together at the end of the tunnel. "After we left Area 51, we came here, but I was fully sedated the whole time. I can't guess what's behind the door any more than you can. It's one thing to be aware of things unknown to most and quite another to be experiencing it live."

"I know," Jules whispered. "My knees are weak, and it's not just from the ride." When she spoke, she pleasantly realized she was already hearing normally.

It usually took her hours after an aircraft ride.

"I don't remember anything about this place from the birthing adventure either," Noah continued. "Miriam told me that right after I was born, the Sky Scanner simply did a stork delivery to her."

When the door opened, two women sporting perfect smiles and garbed in medical coats greeted them. The women were absolutely identical down to their last eyelash.

One of the women said matter-of-factly, "You two look rather beat up, scrappy, and certainly days away from your last shower."

The second woman nodded her agreement and added, "Not to judge. We'll get you back in shape after we formally check the necklaces and the paperwork on the both of you."

Jules hesitated, trying to think of a polite way to inquire if they were clones.

Both women started to laugh. "Let me guess," one of them said to Jules. "You think we are clones. All the new arrivals think that. We are identical twins, born in In Cleveland, Ohio. We are humans who were rescued two years ago. We arrived beat up and looking pretty scrappy, too."

The attendants began to analyze the necklaces and pulled the matching file folders.

Before they parted to separate desks for their interviews, Noah smiled and whispered to Jules, "I think we have an excellent chance of blending in. Look, see, they use regular manilla file folders. That makes me feel a little better. Anyway, it's a shred of something that we do back home."

"We can compare notes later. I still am feeling somewhat skeptical," Jules replied.

Noah and Jules were directed to separate desks, each with one of the twin attendants.

At the end of her interview, Jules was advised, "You are so welcome here as a new teacher. Miriam has highly recommended you, and we all value her opinion greatly. In a moment, we will take you both to be decontaminated. There are two separate chambers. One of us will walk through one of the chambers with each of you. Since we welcomed you before you both were decontaminated, we also require the decontamination process."

Noah's interview was wrapping up. Their voices were raised enough for Jules and her attendant to hear the ongoing conversation.

Noah's attendant had grown enthusiastic. "I can't believe I finally got the chance to meet a real spy!" she said.

Noah stubbornly tried to explain. "No. Not a spy like you think of the occupation. Think of it as my having been a fly. You know, like a house fly on the wall who buzzes back information."

"It seems that you are heavily burdened with the concept of humility. Don't try to make light of all your fine efforts. It's healthy to feel some pride," the attendant replied, her voice obviously dripping with adoration. "Being a spy is an approved occupation on my list, but you can ask to do any posted jobs that interest you. I can't imagine anyone wanting to do a job less exciting than spying."

"I can imagine wanting calmer employment," Noah countered. "I've been on Earth for one hundred eight years. Have you lived that long? Believe me. I'm old enough to know when enough is enough. I got away before the fly got a swatting, and I intend to keep it that way. Currently, my aspiration is to lead a normal, productive life."

Jules' attendant cleared her throat and interjected, "Sis?" She then gave her sister a cautionary nod.

"Well, all right, if you insist," Noah's attendant said with a heavy sigh. "I will put down that you are undecided on your new occupation. That way, if you change your mind about being a spy, you can still apply for that job."

"Perfect," Noah said with a tired smile.

CHAPTER TWENTY—FOUR

The twin attendants escorted Noah and Jules to the decontamination area behind a door adjacent to their interview room.

Jules' attendant took control of any of the further directions needed. "Due to exposure to Earth and other arrivals, the attendants and the arrivals both need to move through a painless decontamination process. We will step up on a conveyor that will coast you through the chamber. Do not be concerned if sensors cause it to stop and start as needed, depending on what type of momentary contamination unfolds. Take your backpacks with you. Afterward, we will send them over to Bill and Miriam's accommodations.

"What awaits you at the end of the chamber is a door that will open onto the long-awaited shower reception room. At that point in time, you will part ways with your interview attendants. You each will have separate shower rooms to enable you to shower for as long as you desire.

"Fresh, clean, casual clothing items have already been prepared for your redressing. Your clothing can be worn into the decontamination chamber, but it is torn and stained. For that reason, we are unable to salvage the items. We will take care of the disposal of your current clothing."

Noah noticed a large sink and mirror in the corner of the room. "Before decontamination, could we trouble you to allow Jules and I to use the mirror and take a last look at our dust covered earthly selves?"

"Brace yourselves a bit before you take a look, but be our guests," the attendant replied.

"Come on, Jules. Don't worry. Unlike me, you only look sweetly soiled," Noah said as he grabbed her hand and ushered her into the corner by the sink.

The mirror proved to reveal them both in a far less than glorious reflection. Jules' face was streaked with sweat and dirt, but some had been wiped clean when she sheltered herself under Noah's wet armpit. Noah was so thickly laden with dirt that the whites of his eyes proved an impressive addition to his face. His hair was still partially spiked. They were indeed crumpled versions of themselves. They stared at the mirror in disbelief for a moment before Noah turned Jules toward him and brushed several loose strands of hair from her face.

"Don't you think we should immortalize our last earthy and Earthling moment? I sort of feel like this is New Year's Eve for us. I want to kiss my old life goodbye and then kiss in a new life. Will you help me? I'm finding the need to know if a kiss varies before and after decontamination. Are you equally curious?"

"You should consider salesman as a new occupation," Jules murmured. They both lost themselves in a tender first kiss.

One of the attendants looked pleased. "Let's continue with the experiment!" she said. "Decontamination awaits!"

Her twin was silent but exhibiting a slight pout.

The decontamination ride hummed under their feet, creating a slight vibration, but it took little if any, time. They all arrived together at the shower reception area. Jules and Noah both immediately gave the shower rooms a yearning glance.

"We should continue the test," Noah reminded her. We can do one before the showers and one after if you choose to. We might as well seek full, rounded results to analyze," he said with a hopeful look in his eyes.

"Ever onward with your fascinating experiment," Jules remarked just before they embarked on another more lingering kiss.

"See you for one more after we shower. Maybe you won't recognize me, but the fact that we are the only ones taking showers at the moment should prove helpful," Noah whispered before they parted ways.

"Scoot, you two," an attendant said. "You both have that lingering aroma of venom on you."

The shower felt gloriously wonderful and beyond Jules' wildest dreams. She felt no desire to rush away from the fresh, warm water that streamed over her body and revived her. The water lacked the dense chemical smell she had become all too familiar with. This shower felt like a continuous warm caress.

A back brush extended itself. It worked its way up and down her back as she stood there. "So, where have you been all my life?" Jules murmured. She could see she was shedding some caked dust from her hair as she washed it three times, just to be sure. Even in her sandbox days, she had never become coated in soil as much as she had gained during their adventure while they journeyed through the dank old tunnel.

Jules imagined Noah's shower floor was quite the picture of darker brown water circling the drain. It was not only clever but interesting how Noah had managed to extract kisses from her. She sensed that Noah thought they should run things out and go for broke concerning Gabe's new mom fantasy. It would ring true or not, which would settle the issue about her being Gabe's candidate. The two of them could afford the time to resolve the issue. They would end up as just friends or much more than that. It was theirs to find the answer. Sooner or later, her heart would speak about the matter, and so would Noah's.

Drying after her shower reminded Jules of the car wash back home, with the exception that the wind blew in a much gentler vein. Her new set of clothing was neatly folded in the shower's anti-room. It was a lighter-weight summer style, similar to what Jules inadvertently had left behind for the town to sell.

She would likely never see the beauty of the four seasons again until reassigned for Earth's clean-up. Jules hadn't raked for three days, and she didn't miss it one iota. As a trailing thought, Jules hoped Peter had made it over to Carrie's place. If the government did spring a quick entry into Military Law, she hoped Peter was at Carrie's when it happened.

Jules emerged from her shower room to find a clean, polished version of Noah Verne, complete with a broad smile. She could sense that he was ready for the final test kiss.

"My, Dear," Noah remarked. "You certainly clean up well."

"And Sir, so do you," was Jules' response as they leaned into the third test kiss. This time, Jules' heart seemed to skip a beat. Shortly thereafter, Noah bent down and quickly kissed her forehead. "Nice stuff," he murmured.

A voice broke the silence. Two new attendants had been standing there the entire time. "What are the kiss test results?" one of them inquired.

"We haven't had time to discuss and produce a report covering the details as yet," Noah commented as he gazed into Jules' sparkling blue eyes. "We need a day or so to complete documentation on the experiment. Then, I think we will be happy to share our results."

"Yes," Jules agreed. "I think we need a day or two to detail things out."

The attendant nodded in good humor. "Both of you are scheduled for physical analysis, which must be done separately. The sooner we complete that part of your welcome package, the sooner you will reunite for food, socialization, and, well, other things you might enjoy."

"Do you have coffee here?" Both Jules and Noah asked in unison.

"Most certainly, The attendant answered. "Once you are health scanned, you can sit down in our spa area. We can serve that to you while discussing what is available here at Peaceful Waters. You can opt for a massage while we answer questions you may have." Your mini apartments will be ready and assigned by the time we have completed the introduction. Assuming you are not ill or injured, the procedure is not lengthy. We are curious about the kiss test results and look forward to your report."

Noah squeezed Jules' hand. "See you later," he called back as he left with his attendant.

CHAPTER TWENTY-FIVE

Jules' medical technician greeted her once she entered the examination room. "My name is Yuni. Please remove all clothing in preparation for a quick bright light scan. It is a record of your skeletal structure and reveals any abnormalities that need to be corrected."

Jules complied. The scan was done in a flash and quickly taken as if it were just a photo. Immediately afterward, Jules was slipped into a light cotton robe and ushered onto an examination table. The complicated equipment surrounding the table initially made Jules feel a bit leery, but sensors were built into the table, and a further detailed internal body scan was accomplished without invasive techniques.

"Don't feel nervous. A lot of the equipment you see is for surgeries only." Yuni mentioned when she noticed Jules was wary. "Your bone construction shows no abnormalities, but the table scan reveals a tendency for allergic reactions. The table is repairing your immune system and will complete that work in a moment."

Jules closed her eyes and pushed away any remaining apprehension by concentrating on the image of a day spa and focusing on coffee as her reward.

"Relax as best you can while I massage you to repair all your cuts, bruises, and sore muscles. I am working as fast as I can because I heard you asked for coffee, and I know what a deprived feeling that can create. Three days with no coffee? You are a poor, suffering soul."

The concept of finally being allergy-free delighted Jules. She could feel the sensors creating a light vibration echo throughout her body. The massage relieved all her physical discomforts. By the time she was given back her clothing, she noticed that all her bruises and cuts had healed with only the touch of Yuni's hands.

"I'm surprised how closely the clothes I was given look like what I wore on Earth," Jules mentioned as she dressed.

Yuni explained, "Anyone coming or going from the base is always dressed to blend in upon landing. I can hear the coffee wagon approaching. I will definitely enjoy several cups with you. Come sit down over in the adjacent lounge area."

Once they were both sunk deeply into the comfortable leather chairs, Yuni continued. "The scanner's Commander wishes to apologize for the rough transport. It's unusual for him to discharge any weapons or avoid crossfire. Your group was the first to arrive. Once he became aware that incomers were stranded and waiting, he had to use the cargo delivery ships for transport."

"Tell him thank you. That is considerate of him. No one was injured during the flight. I am so grateful for the rescue and its timing; we all are." Jules replied.

"The young boy that came along with your group had several broken bones. He also had come in contact with venom, although not seriously. He has lost his parents and siblings. He will need some medical and emotional support, but we expect full recovery. He was in shock and unable to speak, but he was very grateful for his rescue. It will be several weeks before you see him again. His necklace gave us the information we needed for identification. We were glad to have access to it."

"You can heal with your hands like Miriam," Jules mentioned as she was handed a mug of fresh coffee. "Wait a minute. Is it my imagination, or is this Tim Hortons coffee?"

"Is there any other?" Yuni said, smiling. "We do business with Tim Hortons in Canada. The Coffee Shops and ice rinks are still open up there.

"I am a healer, which is a gift all Star Ones have," Yuni continued.

"Exactly where am I?" Jules asked.

"You are in the Golden Triangle Area, at a safe haven known as Peaceful Waters, which also has many underground locations. Our location stretches underneath Lake Ontario, part of Lake Erie, continues up and under Toronto, and connects to our research facility deep under the Finger Lakes on the south side. Peaceful Waters has under-ocean bases, too.

"This complex is built on multiple levels. Including all levels of the base, we can house and sustain a population of over a million residents. We are nearly self-sufficient, and we train our residents in methods of sustainable manufacture of goods, animal husbandry, agriculture, and all of the building trades.

"Each of our locations around the world functions as an ark. Each ark area is expansive, with numerous little towns and villages all tucked safely into the Earth. We house growing samplings of every plant and animal from the respective country where a particular base is located.

"Our population is a mix of races, meaning our pure Star Ones, humans such as yourself, and those of various combinations of the two, such as Special Offspring and Star Children. All are treated equally here but have various levels of gifts. The original Star Ones have life extension accomplished by duplication, as do the descendants of the original Star Ones who were the founders of our civilization. We also house some talented human duplicates."

"Where did the original Star Ones come from?" Jules asked as she refilled their mugs with coffee.

"From Old Russia, as they call it. They settled there in ancient times after their planet became uninhabitable. In between, the remains of their people lived on a Star Cruiser.

"Even as the Star Ones built Old Russia into an astounding civilization, the predecessors of the same hostile forces in place today were scheming to destroy every last Star One, desecrate all we had achieved, steal our technology, and leave no trace of our existence. They did accomplish most of that and even wiped our memory off the history of planet Earth.

"But some of us were fortunate enough to escape the genocide. It was slow going, but after many years, there were enough of us to build back on Earth. However, this time around, we kept it primarily underground and mostly underwater. We finally have some bold Star Ones, Star Children, and Special Offspring, who walk unnoticed among the humans on Earth."

"Russia still exists today. Isn't Old Russia part of the current existing Russia?" Jules asked.

"In a way, but Old Russia was a way more extensive area. It even had settlements in North America. The current Russian Government has been given our true history. In good time, they will release it, and hopefully, they will invite us back. We no longer want a large country with borders to defend. We would like small Towns and Villages dotted here and there.

Places where we could train youth to build beautiful buildings for all to admire. Places where goodwill shines forth daily.

"Ask Miriam and Bill to tell you their story. They won't just mention it to you. Ask Miriam directly about her life in Old Russia, which is the current terminology used to identify the past civilization. Because of the deep sadness concerning its loss, no one refers to the place as Grand Tartaria. It is too painful for the Star Ones."

Jules had only heard that name mentioned once before. It happened when they were planting spring bulbs at the Town Park. Carrie had plunked her box of bulbs on the ground and told them, "This place is a far cry from Grand Tartaria, but I guess you'll have to grow where you're planted."

"Were you born at Peaceful Waters?" Jules asked.

"No, on the Star Cruiser," she said. Years ago, I came to Peaceful Waters along with my parents. They had a job assignment regarding the preparation for this migration. We expanded all of our underground facilities at that time, and since then, we have always been preparing for what has now come to pass.

"We have correspondents sending us news from above ground. The reptilians plan to take full advantage of the pending food tragedy, but if all goes goes as we foresee, within a relatively short period of time, the struggle will finally be over."

"What do you foresee will happen?" Jules asked.

Yuni answered with confidence in her words. "The new food is eventually terminal to humans, but same-day demise awaits reptilians who feed on any human who has consumed the new artificial food. Since elites and their followers will be eating real food, they will quickly become the prime source of food for the reptilians. As the reptilians realize their food supply is diminishing, they will opt to vacate Earth. A few may succeed, but none will be able to return.

"We organized a program called 'Bountiful Harvest'. We doubled our harvest this year. We are establishing safe drop-off places where healthy foodstuffs will be directly doled out to humans by Star Ones who have the gift of smelling any waft of deceit in the air.

"You were fortunate to immediately begin your migration here even before we sent word to do so. We sent our ships out looking for our incoming people. In the following weeks many more are expected to come here.

"Your government sealed the tunnel under the Niagara River when we reached no agreement to assist them in the way that was being demanded of us. In the process of filling the tunnel, they damaged one of our entrances to our base.

"We are fully protecting our air space now with visible craft. We consider the damage to our base an act of war. We have systematically disengaged all the stockpiled significant weaponry on Earth. It is our way of avoiding a massive conflict. We are hunting down the balance of their concealed weapons. We do not threaten, but we do take necessary action when needed.

"All of the underground safe havens the aggressors built and the military tunnels connecting their bases are now closed to them. They will have to struggle and suffer as they intended only the ordinary humans should do.

"You are very safe here, and I am sure our time to begin helping extensively will begin soon. Meanwhile, there is much for you to learn and a lot to accomplish.

"There is a hologram room called Tranquility Hall. You seem to be sitting in a meadow under a sunny blue sky. The Star Ones recharge themselves in the sunlight there, but others simply feel the need to remember being above ground. It is a popular picnic place. You will find we share many of your customs. In the far past we originated most of your customs.

"I will continue to be available to introduce you to areas on the base and help you settle into your new surroundings, but I am sure Bill and Miriam will give you a guided tour. You can contact me on your room phone." She gave Jules a business card. "Any immediate questions?" She asked.

"What about clones?" Jules asked. "Are there many of those?"

"None here at all. We use a rebirth method to extend a life. That is an accepted way of extending a natural limited life span. We believe it is an excellent option for those who pursue knowledge and are of peaceful temperament. Earth is where more cloning is prevalent than ordinary people realize. But there, it is done to continue power and position and not to achieve the betterment of all.

"A man in your arrival party is a duplicate via rebirth. He was an approved situation to help our quest to deter the complete destruction of the planet. I guess you could think of what we developed years ago as a sort of secret agent program," Yuri said with a warm smile.

"Bill and Gabe are waiting beyond that exit door. You can blow your hair dry if you like but it is nearly dry and looks very lovely as it is. This is what you would call a healing spa. You are welcome to come here anytime. You can ask for me if you choose to do so."

"If you choose," Jules said, "is a phrase I haven't heard in a few years."

"I know what you are saying," Yuni replied. "We don't want you to be homesick. It's not yet safe for you there. If you truly want to return, discuss it with Miriam or Bill. We have Comfort Rooms available where your memories of where you lived are projected around you. It can help you ease the adjustment should you find the need."

Jules could understand that despite the turmoil, for some, homesickness could set in. "You've made me feel quite welcome, Yuni. Things had just taken a dietary turn for the worse. We had a direct confrontation with reptilians in order to get here. I don't think my wanting to return is currently a great desire of mine." Jules replied. "I'm enthused over the rebuilding aspect. I quite like Miriam, and I'm looking forward to being further educated by her."

"I'm sure you will. She is heavily involved in both current education and education concerning the past. She is interesting to all of us," Yuni replied.

"Miriam has a history of teaching a class called 'How to Acquire a Sense of Humor.' She has made a serious study of it. All humans, Special Offspring, and Star Children are born with a sense of humor, although there are various levels. It's something genetic to humans that the Star Ones have to be inspired about and then practice. Humor eases difficulties, is very therapeutic, and helps us communicate well with humans. Watching Star One's fumble to learn humor is like watching a great comedy. Ask to assist at one of her classes. You'll see exactly what I mean."

The environment Jules was coming from had left little room for laughter. "I'm afraid laughter was siphoned out of the human race the first year of the United World Nation takeover. Some of the youngest children have never heard the sound of laughter. I'll be sure to make it a point to ask to assist her because it may help me work with transition children."

Jules pushed away thoughts about the oppression that had become so prevalent within Earth's social structure. She felt relaxed and renewed. Oddly, it was as if the dark memories of the past few years were fading. A new comforting kind of usual that spoke of future possibilities now seemed to surround her.

CHAPTER TWENTY-SIX

Jules stood waiting for the exit door to open. Scarcely a second passed before Jules' heart began to race. She became suspicious that she was dreaming and felt her stomach tighten. She couldn't remember blacking out, but maybe she had. Things had turned unbelievable once she descended her basement stairs. It was possible that she had fallen and was unconscious. Perhaps she had contrived a dream that focused on escaping her surroundings to strive to ease the confines of the world she lived in.

Jules broke into a sudden sweat, terrified of what she would wake up to and see around her. Had they sent her to the unidentified somewhere? Standing in front of a door seemed far too symbolic for her to be waiting to see a new future unfold. Tears came to her eyes, and her body began to quake.

Yuni stepped up behind her and put her hand on Jules' shoulder. "Jules, everything is fine. I delayed the door opening because I knew you would feel a tinge of adjustment panic. Everyone does. When you feel ready, I will open the door."

Jules took a deep breath. "Am I really safe now? I was thinking I might be dreaming this up and laying unconscious in my basement."

Yuni laughed. "You are really here, and may I add, it looked like you passed the decontamination kiss with flying colors. That seemed pretty real to me. I nearly forgot. Here is your cantaloupe back. We fully ripened it for you."

"It may take some time to get used to openly communicating with strangers, but it is the best thing to do if you feel on edge. There will be an adjustment period, but having your friends and making new friends will help you through it."

Jules examined the cantaloupe in its fully ripened glory. "It smells so delightful."

Yuni looked her in the eye. "Dreams don't include a sense of smell. So, now. Shall I open the door?"

"Yes. Please do," Jules answered.

Outside of the exit door, Bill and Gabe were patiently waiting.

"There you are, and looking the new, improved version of yourself, may I add," Bill said. "Noah disappeared, questing after coffee. He'll catch up to us.

"Miriam is waiting in Tranquility Hall." Bill continued. "She aims to recharge herself until she feels and looks a thousand years younger, but the rest of us are planning on my dragging her out of there so we can find buffet dining."

Bill led them to the Tranquility Hall entrance. "I'll bring her out of there. Don't go in right now, or you'll all get engrossed and dally around pleasantly distracted for many hours." Bill simply opened the door and whistled. Miriam promptly emerged from Tranquility Hall.

"By the way," Gabe told Bill, "Nemo was examined before his luxury treatment. Everyone is amazed by your expertise. Right off, I made sure that they all knew not to soak him in water. They'll find out soon enough that Nemo frowns on any lengthy grooming, but he is feasting on their flattery."

When she had emerged, Miriam looked entirely revitalized and had regained her energy and enthusiasm. Together, they all proceeded to walk down the hallway.

Happiness exuded from every inch of Miriam as she took Bill's hand while they walked together. "It's so good to be home," Miriam shared with all of them. "What I love about this place is that they keep you connected to Earth because our mission is reliving on Earth. We play Earth sports in our stadiums. We have great dining, cultivate, and raise our own food supply, and now, via Sky Scanner delivery, we are beginning to supply products to the Earth's surface markets. Cloaking our crafts for that maneuver is still imperative. Humans have begun to use drones for delivery, but we can get our products to market a whole lot faster."

As they walked on and on, Miriam chatted. She was back to her same old, energetic self. "Years ago, we used to bring food in sometimes. Remember going out for takeout, Bill?" Miriam asked. "People were so busy watching the decoy ships in the sky that it was pretty easy to land behind the crowd and to go right into the restaurant and order to go. No lines."

Bill shook his head. "Miriam, after all we've just been through, don't even think about any trip out for a pizza at this juncture. I imagine that by now, they have made the restaurants and pizza shops off-limits to regular citizens. In Buffalo, that is going to quickly bring in the need for martial law. All they really had to do to cut available protein was reduce the number of pepperoni pieces allowed on a large pizza to, let's say, five only, and the Western New York riots would absolutely begin raging. I told you before. It's time we teach them to make a good pizza right here. Considering the amount of time we lived in the Buffalo, NY area, we certainly taste-tested enough to know the proper score."

"Bill, you know I'm a firm believer in fine traditions," Miriam firmly stated. "Buffalo should be rebuilt as a shining example of what perseverance can accomplish. I'm going to suggest that we borrow some of the restaurant equipment from the closed shops and be prepared to deliver warm pizza, wings, calzones, and sub sandwiches. A warm local-style meal drop shipped after we finish each day of reconstruction will be more than welcomed and a fine extension of our friendship."

As they turned a corner, they found themselves in an area lined with quaint little shops filled with fascinating handmade merchandise. A canopied, bright red flower cart caught Jules' eye. Noah was obviously engaged in a conversation with the cart vendor. As Noah moved aside, Jules caught sight of the girl who was assisting him. Jules immediately sped over to the cart. "Carrie?" she said, half lost in disbelief.

Everyone stopped and waited to see what had attracted Jules' attention.

"Jules!" Carrie responded as she stepped away from the cart and hugged Jules a welcome. "Now my day is complete. Meet me at the flower cart tomorrow at lunchtime.

"Peter," Carrie called. "I can't believe it. Look who just arrived!" Peter popped his head out from under the cart where he was tightening up a wheel. "Hey, it's Jules. I bet that long about now that snoty AI at Five Star sure is missing our expertise. They have little factories here. I asked them to check out Jim and his family and see if they qualify for quick transport so they can contribute to the cause."

Jules turned to Noah. "It's crazy to find old friends here. Did you find your beloved cup of brew?"

"I sure did. Carrie and I just happened to find a little something to celebrate the return of the credentials of the Teacher of the Talking Flowers."

Noah presented Jules with a sweet bouquet of pink and white snapdragons wrapped in pink paper and tied with a little red bow. Be My Valentine.

"Thank you both so much!" Jules said. "What a wonderful day. It's true. I'm free to be a Teacher again; my credentials are fully restored."

Noah took Jules' hand. "May I?" he asked as they began to move back to where their group was waiting. "I must say, you certainly look more charming than any teacher that graced a classroom I was in. I hope you aren't fluffed about how I maneuvered those three kisses. I'll feel nervous until you say that you enjoyed them as much as I did, or perhaps I'll be saddened because all you will say is that I have your forgiveness."

Jules squeezed his hand. "Who am I to harshly judge such resourcefulness?"

At that precise moment, her heart whispered to her, "Take a chance."

Jules and Noah stopped walking down the hall. She looked deeply into Noah's eyes and boldly replied, "Truthfully? The kisses worked like kindling." She could see elation flash across Noah's face.

"Well then, as a welcome, they sent a bottle of wine and several James Bond films to my room. I really had to snicker," he said to Jules. "Those movies are far from my everyday chance-taking adventures, except for that Area 51 exit. At some point, I will have to set that record straight around here."

"I wouldn't mind watching a film or two if we can locate some takeout, popcorn, and most of all, we now know they have Tim Hortons coffee here," Jules responded.

"This will be my first date in my forty-two years, this time around," Noah said with a triumphant smile.

Jules rolled the cantaloupe across the hall floor to Gabe. "Please take care of the baby until morning, then we all can share it."

"I sure will do," Gabe replied.

Jules moved closer to Noah. "You just gave me a gift, and now I owe you one."

"Yes. You owe me one, according to our understanding," Noah agreed.

Jules put her arms around his neck and lifted her head. Her face wore a sweet, secretive smile as she whispered, "Pile one on me, Sugar." The fourth breathless kiss found its mark and circled their hearts.

Cheers echoed up and down the hall. "Yes, finally. The possibilities increase as the public displays continue!" Gabe exclaimed. "Yes, yes, and yes again. I heard all about the kiss test. Gossip rumbles right along. Nothing slips by around here."

"Gabe, what are your plans?" Noah asked. "You are certainly welcome to join us if you like," he added quickly.

"No, no, and no," Gabe quickly declined. "I'll leave you two to your movies, your moves, and let nature continue to take its course. I'm having my first date at age fifty-eight. I think it's long overdue. My attendant offered to take me to experience the space ride simulator. She said it was far more comfortable than the cargo hold, and it would help Nemo overcome his fears. After that, all three of us go to a late-night, fast played, Star Ones soccer game. I think my dream of learning and then getting in a few high speed soccer games might come to be a reality for me here. I'll get all the information about that tonight. How do we pay for, you know, stuff?"

"We are sort of on a free ride at the moment. We barter our help and talents," Bill answered. "Believe me, we will be more than paying our way once we begin helping to rebuild civilization on Earth. It's going to be a long, hard haul to turn things back around, let alone improve them. Redemption never comes easy."

Miriam's showed another surge of energy. "I, for one, could tell you all some wild stories about helping my parents after the great flood. Bill, you should have seen that mess. Once the waters began receding, it was a blessing that the past was buried underground. This time, the debris cleanup is going to be awfully challenging." Miriam paused and looked at the amazement on everyone's face, including Bill's. "Rest assured, that was my version of a well-deserved joke concerning my age. Please, stop guessing at my age."

But Gabe had already run the calculation through in his head. He turned to his father and Jules and mouthed a silent, wide-eyed, "Wow, can that be a real truth?"

"Gabe, I don't think it wise to point fingers about age," Noah laughed, "It's a strange world when a son is older than his father but still the son of his father. Now, isn't it?"

Gabe laughed delightedly, "That one could throw all those tracing ancestry a curve that would turn into an eternal loop."

"True," Nemo said as he caught up behind them. Every Kevlar strand was combed perfectly in place until he stopped momentarily and shook himself. Nemo disliked wearing a collar, but somehow, someone had convinced him to wear a "Peaceful Waters" medallion on a ribbon around his neck since he had already endeared himself to many hearts and become a celebrity.

Nemo sat down for a moment. Looking content and clearly pleased, he raised his head. "Proud," he said in a clearly determined fashion.

Bill laughed, "There you go. The Captain has happily leaned into his new environment and even learned a brand new word."

ABOUT THE AUTHOR

Although a native of Western New York for most of her life, the author of this book also resided for ten years in a cabin deep in the bowels of Appalachian coal-mining country, close to nature, on the edge of Braddock's Run and adjacent to the wilderness of Savage Mountain. Her respect for nature deepened there.

The immediate area hosted a wide array of diversified individuals. The local area also boasted interesting descendants of General Custer, John Wilkes Booth, and a few of Lizzie Borden's family relations. It was a well-learned lesson concerning how formidable wildlife, nature, and individuals can be.

If not set in unspecific locations, her books begin in Buffalo, New York, an area rich with past history and offering numerous impressive settings. They then travel on to encompass other regions of America or a foreign country.

The author gardens profusely, wintering many plants in her home with an attached greenhouse. She finds that writing fiction is similar to gardening. Some characters planted in a novel are allowed to flourish, some only fill in the necessary groundwork, and some are fated to die on the vine. Sometimes, nurturing a character requires intense hoeing.

The author's fictional writing interests range from adventure in the ancient past or current times in a world seasoned in various degrees with aliens or spiritual adversaries. Following the lead of whatever inspires her, the author adheres to the principle that the reader deserves a good ride. The author's unfinished stories reside in a folder entitled "Spits in the Wind".